Fantasies
Pamela Wallace

Silhouette Intimate Moments
Published by Silhouette Books New York
America's Publisher of Contemporary Romance

Other Silhouette Books by Pamela Wallace

Come Back, My Love
Love with a Perfect Stranger
Dreams Lost, Dreams Found

 SILHOUETTE BOOKS, a Division of Simon & Schuster, Inc.
1230 Avenue of the Americas, New York, N.Y. 10020

ISBN: 0-671-46204-0

First Silhouette Books printing October, 1983

10 9 8 7 6 5 4 3 2 1

America's Publisher of Contemporary Romance

Printed in the U.S.A.

Spence Leaned Closer, and Devon Waited, Scarcely Breathing.

Then, suddenly, she caught herself and drew away, not so much physically as emotionally. *Be careful,* she told herself. *Remember who you are, who he is.*

Everything about this man pulled her to him. Like the ocean, he could be serene and calm. But he could also be dangerous and terrifying.

The sun disappeared below the horizon. When they were almost back to Spence's house, Devon turned to look back. There was the barest beginning of a new moon. "There," she said, pointing, "is poetic imagery. That's my idea of a beautiful promise."

Spence looked at the moon, then at her, and Devon wished this could go on forever. This tranquil mood. No arguments. No intrusions.

Fantasy time.

Dear Reader:

Silhouette has always tried to give you exactly what you want. When you asked for increased realism, deeper characterization and greater length, we brought you Silhouette Special Editions. When you asked for increased sensuality, we brought you Silhouette Desire. Now you ask for books with the length and depth of Special Editions, the sensuality of Desire, but with something else besides, something that no one else offers. Now we bring you SILHOUETTE INTIMATE MOMENTS, true romance novels, longer than the usual, with all the depth that length requires. More sensuous than the usual, with characters whose maturity matches that sensuality. Books with the ingredient no one else has tapped: excitement.

There is an electricity between two people in love that makes everything they do magic, larger than life—and this is what we bring you in SILHOUETTE INTIMATE MOMENTS. Look for them wherever you buy books.

These books are for the woman who wants more than she has ever had before. These books are for you. As always, we look forward to your comments and suggestions. You can write to me at the address below:

Karen Solem
Editor-in-Chief
Silhouette Books
P.O. Box 769
New York, N.Y. 10019

To my sisters,
Robin Corrales and Jeanne Aldridge,
with love

Fantasies

Chapter 1

DEVON O'NEILL DROVE HER PALE BLUE AUSTIN HEALEY convertible—a low-slung, beautifully restored classic— up to the front gate of United Film Studios. At thirty-four Devon was still often mistaken for just another pretty starlet. Her mahogany hair shimmered darkly in the cool, crisp October sunshine, her olive complexion was flawless, and her blue eyes were a vivid cerulean fringed with thick, sooty lashes.

But she wasn't a starlet. She was the brand-new president of the studio, and shortly everyone would know it.

"Name, please," the guard in the tiny cubicle asked perfunctorily.

When Devon responded, he checked it on his list of people approved to enter the lot. A look of surprise transformed his bored expression. "Harrison Kahn cleared you?" he asked.

Devon nodded. Harrison was the owner of the studio, and his name had the power to impress a great many more people than the guard. As he pushed the button that raised the bar blocking the way, the guard looked at Devon with unabashed curiosity. She smiled in return, and drove onto the lot.

Harrison had interviewed her and hired her that very weekend. In one hectic trip to his headquarters in New York she had gone from being a successful production vice-president to being the second woman ever to run a motion picture studio.

A flashing red warning light caused traffic to back up. Devon stopped her car and waited for the light to go off. Beyond her a scene was being shot. A second assistant director stood near the light, talking into a walkie-talkie. In the distance the shoot was in progress. There was a cluster of people, actors in police uniforms, a director riding with a Panaflex camera mounted on a crane.

With a rueful smile Devon remembered her own days as a second assistant director. It was a job fraught with headaches, for the second AD was responsible for getting people and equipment together to spare the director the mundane chore of doing so.

In a moment the scene was completed and the red light went off. Traffic moved ahead. As Devon passed the permanent sets—Western streets, city blocks, and small-town neighborhoods—she felt a sense of homecoming. She had been on the lot often as a child. Her mother, Sheila O'Neill, had been a major movie star from the late 1940's to the early 1960's and had made many movies there.

Devon grew up surrounded by the movie business; a movie set was a second home to her. Consequently there was very little she didn't know about the industry.

Looking around now, Devon thought how little the lot had changed since she was a child. It was still, like all studios, a factory. The rows of dull gray office buildings and ugly, massive sound stages attested to that. But it was a factory that produced fantasies. Already Devon felt a thrill of excitement at the thought of having the tremendous resources of the studio at her disposal.

She parked her car in an empty space marked *Leif* in front of the executive office building. Jack Leif had been the president of this studio. Now Devon was taking his place. Picking up her slim leather briefcase, she headed toward the building.

"Hey, lady, that's reserved for the studio president," a young messenger shouted at her as he rode past on a bicycle.

"Yes. I know," Devon replied with a grin, then continued walking.

I made it, she thought. And I didn't have to sleep with anyone or step on anyone to get here.

After years of working her way up the ladder, Devon had finally achieved the power that in Hollywood was almost always reserved for men. The launching pad, she knew, was her work on *Lovelorn,* a romantic comedy that had grossed one hundred million dollars. After her work on that picture she'd expected a promotion. When it didn't materialize, she took a hard look at her situation. She could recognize a brick wall when she saw one. She quit, determined to find a studio that wouldn't hold her back simply because she was a woman. She knew it would be difficult; the middle-management level of Hollywood was saturated with women, but the top was an almost exclusively male preserve. Nevertheless she was determined to succeed despite the odds.

She'd been on her own only one week when Harrison dangled the presidency of United Film Studios in front of her.

Remembering her interview with Harrison after a last-minute flight to New York, Devon smiled.

Boy, was I nervous! she thought. When he'd summarily dismissed her degree in film arts from UCLA by saying, "Film students know what they *should* like, not what they *do* like," she'd replied firmly, "I know exactly what I like. I like to laugh. I like to cry. And when I walk out of a theater, I *don't* like to feel I've been cheated. But what I don't like most of all is to see pictures that I've been associated with lose money."

To her relief he'd laughed. She knew then that she had the job.

In Leif's outer office Devon found a confused-looking young secretary and a guard with a passive expression on his stoic face. The door to Leif's private office was open, and inside, Devon could see Harrison talking on the telephone.

Looking at him now, Devon remembered the startling news he'd told her when he hired her. "Jack Leif is an embezzler. To the tune of half a million dollars. Only I and my chief accountant know so far. The one thing I don't want is a period of indecision and confusion like Columbia went through during the Begelman scandal. Report to work Monday morning at ten. By then Leif will be fired and off the lot."

Looking at the nervous expression on the secretary's face and the implacable one on the guard's, Devon had a pretty good idea what kind of scene had just been played out there. She walked up to the secretary and introduced herself.

"Oh! Mr. Kahn said you'd be coming." The girl's voice was tentative. "I'm not sure . . ." she began, then stopped, clearly at a loss as to how to proceed.

She glanced helplessly at the other desk in the anteroom, which was empty. Devon assumed it had belonged to Leif's private secretary, who would have left with him.

Turning back to the young woman, Devon asked, "What's your name?"

"Marci . . . Marci Schoenfeld."

"Have you been here long, Marci?"

"No, Miss O'Neill. In fact this is my first day."

Devon was both amused and relieved. That meant Marci had no feelings of loyalty to Leif, which might have posed a problem. But Devon also couldn't help seeing the humor in the situation. Marci clearly was overwhelmed by the executive suite power play.

After asking some brief questions about Marci's background, Devon decided she could use her as her personal secretary. When she told the girl this, Marci's pale, freckled face broke into a huge grin of relief. Heartfelt thanks were cut short by Harrison, who strode into the room.

He was a short, powerfully built man. Though he was overweight by at least thirty pounds, Devon sensed that in his younger days he had been built like a young bull. Now he was in his late fifties, but his gray-streaked brown hair was still thick. Though he was expensively dressed, there was something of the streetfighter about him in the way his shoulders rolled under his custom-tailored tweed jacket.

Devon knew Kahn was a self-made millionaire. When she met him for the first time, she had been intimidated by the forcefulness of his personality. Now she steeled herself not to let that happen again.

"Morning, Devon. Come on in and we'll get to work."

As Devon followed him into Leif's large office, he continued, "Jack cleared out all his things, so you can settle right in. Later, when there's time, you can redecorate."

Devon glanced quickly at the pristine white walls, navy-blue corduroy sofa and chairs, and glass-topped wooden tables scattered around the room. Then she replied, "This looks fine as it is. I'll just bring in some of my own pictures."

Harrison smiled. His expression had a bit of the hungry alligator about it, but nevertheless there was also a surprising charm.

"Concerned about saving money? Good. Now then," he continued as they sat down at a small table scattered with papers, "I've talked to the publicity department. They're getting out a press release. It will announce Jack's departure—due to 'creative differences'—and your appointment. We're saying nothing about the embezzlement officially. Jack made a lot of money for the studio and I don't want to prosecute. But I don't want him to continue stealing from me either."

Looking at Devon intently, he finished, "You know, there's going to be a lot of press interest in you."

"I know." Devon smiled confidently. "I've been through it before. I can handle it."

She sounded unconcerned, but inside she was less calm than she would let Harrison see. She intensely disliked the fishbowl existence she had known for so long with her mother. Hollywood reporters felt free to pry into the most personal aspects of people's lives if those people were considered newsworthy. Sheila O'Neill, the premier sex goddess of her era, had been considered extremely newsworthy. To this day Devon couldn't face a battery of popping flashbulbs without steeling herself against panicking and running as she had done as a small child.

"Well, I'll let you get on with things, then," Harrison said. "I've phoned just about everyone on the lot who's important to tell them about your appointment. But there's one person I want to talk to personally—Spencer Tait." He gave Devon a shrewd look and finished, "You do know about his position here, don't you?"

She did indeed. Spencer Tait was the most successful

—and, therefore, the most powerful—independent producer working under the UFS umbrella.

She nodded and Harrison explained, "He and Leif are pretty tight. He won't like what's happened. You'll take a lot of heat from that corner. You're going to have to mend fences with him or you won't last long enough to spend your first paycheck."

Devon sat still, considering Harrison's blunt words.

Wonderful, she thought. On top of all the incredible confusion I'm walking into here, I'm handed a built-in feud with a man who probably means more to the studio than I do.

She'd gotten what she always wanted—the opportunity to make movies the way she thought they should be made. But it wasn't going to be the Camelot-like experience she'd envisioned. The lances and maces would be there, but her idealistic dream of finer films would have to await the bloodletting.

Harrison continued, "I expect you to smooth over things with Spence. Technically you're his boss, since the studio finances and releases his pictures. But you understand we want to keep him happy. His movies make a lot of money for us and we don't want him bolting to another studio."

"I understand."

"Good." Harrison rose and headed toward the door. He stopped, turned back toward Devon and finished, "I'm having a party at the Beverly Hills Hotel tonight at eight. I've rented a bungalow there for a couple of days. Every executive from the studio has orders to show up. I'll introduce you to all of them then. In the meantime, get yourself situated here."

When Harrison was gone, Devon moved over to the highbacked leather chair behind the large cherrywood desk. The top of the desk was barren, and Devon knew Leif or his secretary had probably swept off everything into a briefcase or box. She glanced quickly through the drawers but found nothing personal—only odds and ends, like pens, paper clips and notepads with JACK LEIF printed on the top.

She dumped the notepads in the wastebasket, then leaned back in the chair, savoring this special moment. It was utterly quiet and still. From the large window overlooking the lot came only muffled sounds of people and traffic.

Well, I can't sit here basking in my own glory, she told herself. I've got to get to work.

She called Marci in to take some dictation, beginning with a memo asking the heads of the departments to meet with her first thing in the morning. She wanted an overview of every aspect of the studio. Specific producers were asked to provide her with the latest draft scripts of projects the studio had in production or development.

She then dictated another memo introducing herself to every employee of the studio, assuring them she planned no major changes in personnel. She was aware that with the current high unemployment, especially in Hollywood, everyone would be worried about losing his or her job.

She was in the middle of that memo when the door to her office was suddenly thrown open and a man stormed in. Of medium height, with a lean yet muscular build, he had dark blond hair and startling green eyes. His features, which were clouded now by anger, were clean-cut and strong, almost chiseled. He was dressed casually in faded jeans and a green V-neck sweater that showed a tantalizing glimpse of a hard, muscled chest. But despite his casual attire, there was something about him, an aura of quiet but compelling confidence, that indicated he wielded a great deal of power.

Devon recognized him immediately. Spencer Tait. They'd never met, but she had seen his picture in newspapers. And she'd heard a great deal about him, much of it contradictory, all of it fascinating.

Before Devon could say a word, Tait planted himself in front of her desk and began hotly, "What the devil do you think you're doing!"

Turning to a startled Marci, Devon said calmly, "You can go now. And call personnel and tell them to send someone up here to man the other desk."

Marci flashed Devon a grateful smile, then scurried out, clearly relieved to be out of the line of fire.

Leveling a stern look at Tait, Devon answered, "I'm assuming my duties as the new president of this studio. What do *you* think you're doing, bursting in here without so much as a knock?"

"I just talked to Harrison! I don't believe a word he said. Jack Leif is no crook!"

Without asking her permission, he sat down and clasped his hands together between his knees. Making an obvious effort to control his emotions, he repeated more to himself than to her, "Jack Leif is no crook."

Even before Harrison had told her about Tait, Devon had heard of the friendship between Tait and Leif. Leif was the older, experienced mentor, Tait the brilliant protégé. Though Leif had no official credit, it was rumored he had a great deal to do with Tait's Oscar-winning film, *Belle*.

More sorry than angry, Devon searched for a way to ease the awkwardness of this scene. Tait was reputed to be courteous and low-key. She hoped that reputation was accurate.

She began, "I, too, was surprised when—"

"There has to be some other reason why Harrison fired Jack!" Tait interrupted. Suddenly he stopped and studied Devon as if he were just then seeing her. "Why *you?* Jack Leif has been around for years. He's long since paid his dues. Why would Harrison put you in Jack's place?"

Devon wanted to explain that she'd been working her way up, paying her dues too. But his anger threw her. Silently she tried to compose herself. She watched him rise from the chair and walk across the room.

"There was a photograph here, of this lot, taken when Jack first came here."

"Mr. Leif took the photograph with him," Devon responded, still determined to be polite. She told herself that this man was important to the studio.

Damn, she thought, she couldn't even get through her first hour on the job without a major crisis.

Drawing a deep breath to steady her nerves, she continued, "I understand Jack Leif is your friend."

Tait cut her short again. "Damn right he is! But he also happens to be a very good studio chief. He knows more about film than Harrison Kahn and that asinine board of directors of his could ever learn in a lifetime."

Devon knew he was right. The job of studio president was one that few people could handle. It required a thorough knowledge of all pictures in production, as well as input on the development of other projects, advertising, marketing, ad infinitum. The studio chief had to get along well with the creative community, the writers, directors and actors, and at the same time keep these people's costs to a reasonable level.

The myriad, often conflicting responsibilities boggled the mind. Devon certainly had a healthy respect for the difficulties she was facing. But even though Tait was right in praising Leif's abilities, that didn't change the fact of Leif's thievery.

Taking a deep breath, Devon forged ahead bluntly. "The fact remains that Jack Leif stole half a million dollars from this studio." Her tone was even but firm.

"Jack was making a quarter million a year, plus bonuses amounting to at least that much. Why the hell would he steal?"

"You'll have to ask *him* that. Maybe a quarter of a million doesn't go as far as it used to," Devon answered dryly.

Tait paused. Then he said slowly, "Touché."

For just an instant, for the briefest of moments, they looked at each other. In Devon's head, in advanced speed like a crazy comic scene, she saw that this man was someone she could admire. Not too many would fight for a friend who'd been disgraced.

Then the moment passed and his brilliant green eyes, the color of the clearest emerald, narrowed thoughtfully. Devon read him, anticipating the coming question. She wanted to hold up her hands to ward off what was coming. But she knew she couldn't avoid it: It had to be faced. So she sat rigidly, hands folded in her lap, fingers laced tightly.

"Some people are saying you were a surprising choice for studio president. You haven't been around that long."

"What people? How many could you have encountered between your office and mine?"

Her attempt at levity failed. His gaze didn't waver, his tenseness didn't ease.

"What exactly *did* you do, Miss O'Neill, to persuade Harrison to hire you?"

His implication was unmistakable. 'And sordid. Though his voice was deceptively calm, his eyes were flashing angrily.

Devon felt cheated by that previous moment of empathy she'd felt with him. In the few seconds it took to marshal her composure, she told herself she was a fool. She'd come up against this kind of thinking often enough. She shouldn't be surprised. Yet, after all those years in the business, she still felt a stab of intense embarrassment. Especially with *this* man, whose work she so truly admired for its sensitivity, its integrity. For

some unaccountable reason she was terribly disappointed in him. Looking into his eyes, she saw that he, too,
was embarrassed suddenly.

You know better, she thought furiously. Yet, you still
pull the same garbage as any dumb flunkie. Suffused
with a cold fury, she rose slowly, pulling herself up to
the very limit of her five feet eight inches of height so
that she was almost as tall as Tait. Her blue eyes locked
into combat with his piercing green ones.

I could strike him, she thought, but instead she
clenched her hands into tight fists at her sides.

"If your fragile male ego can't handle the fact that a
woman can be capable enough to do this job, that's
your problem, Mr. Tait, not mine! And if you think
Harrison Kahn would jeopardize his business interests
by hiring his mistress, you're stupid as well. You're a
rude, ill-mannered cretin. The next time you want to
see me, make an appointment with my secretary."

Her voice was naturally low. It sank to a whisper with
her next words. "Now—get out."

He hesitated for just a moment. There was a fleeting
change in his angry expression. The green eyes, narrowed in intense dislike, widened in surprise as something more—something nearly like respect—softened
them subtly. Then, without saying a word, he turned
sharply on his heel and went out, slamming the door
behind him.

For several seconds Devon simply stood in the center
of the room, trying to calm down. But her anger and
her hurt went too deep to be easily thrust aside.

Stop it, she told herself firmly. He isn't worth one
moment of unhappiness. He's like every other man in
this town who's terrified a woman might turn out to be
better than he is.

Yet, at the back of her mind she suspected she was
being unfair to him. He wasn't quite like every other
man in Hollywood. He didn't wear gold chains and

white Gucci loafers. He wore faded jeans that fit disturbingly well over the lean hardness of his body.

In fact, she sensed he wasn't like any other man she had ever met before. She suspected there was a great deal more to her intense reaction than mere anger. But that was a possibility she didn't want to dwell on.

Chapter 2

PRECISELY AT EIGHT O'CLOCK THAT EVENING DEVON DROVE
up to the front entrance of the Beverly Hills Hotel. She
had been there often but had never quite grown
accustomed to the hotel's whimsical appearance. It was
salmon pink with white trim and had an ocher-colored
tile roof. Shaded by a variety of trees, including
coconut and date palms, it looked like a set from a
particularly preposterous 1930's musical.

She felt the hotel was strangely appropriate for
Hollywood. It was, after all, an opulent, rather bizarre
fantasy, designed primarily to serve a community that
made its living peddling fantasies.

Inside the surprisingly small, unpretentious lobby
Devon asked the desk clerk which bungalow Harrison
was staying in. When he told her, she recognized the
number. It was the most exclusive of an exclusive set of
bungalows, because it faced Crescent Drive, a quiet
street that bordered the hotel on the east, away from
the noise of Sunset Boulevard. Two minutes later she

was walking past the privet hedges and flowering shrubs that bordered the bungalow and entering its small, Spanish-style walled patio. The door was unlocked and she went in.

The thirty-foot living room was light and cheerful, with white walls, beige carpeting and a walnut fireplace with a crackling fire. The furniture, what Devon could see of it through the dense crowd, was upholstered in bright shades of yellow and green.

The party was already in full swing. Devon couldn't suppress a wry smile at the thought that they had all come early to meet their surprising new boss. Knowing that she would be scrutinized critically, she had dressed in a simple but stunning knee-length red cashmere dress with a modest cowl neck. She'd brushed her thick, shoulder-length hair back from her face. At her ears were exquisite ruby earrings, a gift from her mother.

She wore no other jewelry.

The effect of this simple attire was powerful. The moment she entered the bungalow, heads turned to stare at her, even though many people weren't aware who she was yet.

Devon recognized a few faces, but most of the people were strangers. As she scanned the room she suddenly realized whom she was looking for—Spencer Tait. But he wasn't there. Suppressing her surprising disappointment, she told herself not to be a fool.

Suddenly Harrison called to her from a corner where he was the center of attention in a small group of senior executives. Devon quickly made her way through the crowd to him.

Harrison tersely introduced her to the men around him. She met their welcoming smiles and unabashedly curious looks with a warm, winning smile and a superficial calm that belied the nervousness she felt. The conversation was friendly but slightly guarded. No one mentioned Jack Leif, and everyone deferred to Harrison.

When Harrison left after a few minutes to take a telephone call, Devon took the opportunity to leave the group to mingle with the other guests. Almost immediately a young woman about her own age came up to her.

"Sally!" Devon exclaimed happily, then gave her a warm hug. "Oh, it's so good to see you again. I've been trying to get hold of you for weeks."

Sally laughed sheepishly and replied, "I disappeared for a while. But, Dev, I'm so happy for you!"

"Thanks. I suspect you're the only person in this room who really means it when you congratulate me."

Sally smiled appreciatively. Her hazel eyes sparkled merrily and she tossed her long chestnut hair away from her lovely oval face with a carefully manicured hand.

Looking at her, Devon thought how little Sally had changed since they were roommates at UCLA. Sally had been one of the acknowledged campus beauties then and, if anything, was even more beautiful now that she was more mature. But her beauty wasn't her only asset by any means. She was a magna cum laude graduate with a degree in English literature.

Devon had always respected Sally's ability, especially when it came to analyzing scripts. In fact, she'd half expected Sally to be the one to become head of a studio eventually. But Sally didn't have Devon's determination and drive. There was a fragility about her, a reluctance to make the really hard decisions, that Devon realized now would always keep her from reaching the very top.

Sally continued frankly, "We were all absolutely stunned when we heard the news this morning. The funny thing was that most people didn't know anything about you. 'Who is this dark horse, anyway?' they were all asking. When they heard that I know you, I was besieged with questions. 'What is she like? Is she likely to commit wholesale slaughter and bring in her own people? Is she easy or hard to work with?'"

Devon laughed, relaxing for the first time all day. "What did you tell them? That I'm everyone's nightmare of a vicious woman executive?"

"I was tempted," Sally admitted with a little chuckle. "But I didn't think that would help you get along with them in the long run. So I told them the truth: that you're bright and nice and fair. They can't expect more than that."

"I'm surprised to see you here. The last time we talked you were at Donovan Productions."

"Yes. But after the divorce was final, I had a hard time handling things. So I decided to get away from it all. I went down to Mexico for a while."

Devon's voice softened in concern. "Why didn't you get in touch? I wanted to help."

Sally looked embarrassed. Her glance lowered and she was unable to meet Devon's eyes. "I know. But you couldn't help. No one could. When Jerry walked out, I was shattered."

"You seemed to be getting over it."

"*Seemed* to is right. I was okay as long as I thought there was a chance he would come back. Then I signed the final papers and the next day I heard he was getting married again."

"Oh, Sally, I'm so sorry," Devon responded with heartfelt sympathy. She knew exactly how Sally felt. Her own husband, Tony, a rising young actor, had walked out on her four years earlier. He had left her for a slightly older woman agent who could do his career a great deal of good. Devon had told herself he wasn't worth a single tear, but that didn't stop the tears from falling.

"I'm okay now," Sally reassured Devon. "I came back to Hollywood last month and got this job as UFS—production vice-president. I was going to call you this week."

"Well, congratulations yourself." She smiled and finished, "We're not doing too badly for two idiots who nearly burned down the dorm when we decided to cook on a hibachi in our room."

They both laughed at the memory. It sparked other memories and Devon asked pensively, "Do you remember the first time the 'Old Girls' Network' met?"

Pausing for a moment, Sally said, "Of course. You were running the whole show, as usual. When I asked who elected you mogul, you answered, '*I* did. After all, it's *my* house we're meeting in.'"

Devon smiled, remembering that day ten years earlier. She'd decided that women in Hollywood needed to band together to help each other get past the barriers erected by the men who controlled the business. With characteristic decisiveness she'd immediately formed an organization of all the women she knew working in the film industry. She dubbed it the 'Old Girls' Network' in a parody of the 'Old Boys' Network' that men traditionally used to help each other get ahead.

"You asked me how long it would be before a woman became head of a studio. I said five years."

"And now here you are," Sally responded.

Devon smiled ruefully. "I thought I'd make it by the time I was thirty. That seemed such a long way off then."

"Well, thirty-four isn't so bad. You're only four years off schedule," Sally teased.

"I'm so glad we'll be working together. It will be a tremendous relief to see at least one friendly face in a sea of barracudas," Devon said with a grimace.

"Speaking of that, there's something I want to talk to

you about. Before everyone else closes in with their pet projects."

"What is it?"

"I've got a script. I think it's fantastic, but I can't get anyone here to listen to me."

"I'll listen. What's it about?"

"A remake of *Last Chance*." Sally raised an eyebrow and grinned. "You *do* remember it, don't you?"

"Of course. It was my mother's first big part. She played the role of the daughter."

Devon thought about the film, a classic romantic adventure involving a mother and daughter, the two men they love, and their fight for survival in the wilderness in the mid 1800's. The she said, "And this script has updated the story?"

"Yes. It's exactly the same story line, but the dialogue is harder, more contemporary. Karl Kreiss, the writer-director, did it."

"Kreiss is brilliant. I loved his last film. Why didn't Jack Leif want to do the project?"

"Money. He said it would cost a fortune to shoot it today and he wanted to do a couple of other big-budget films with old cronies of his. You see, the original was shot mainly on sound stages, but Karl wants to do it all on location to give it a more realistic look."

"Sally, I've got a long meeting tomorrow morning, but why don't we have lunch? You can bring a copy of the script. It sounds interesting."

"Great! I just know you'll love it, Dev. And UFS has the rights to the story, so there's no problem there."

While Devon was talking to Sally, suddenly her eye was caught by a latecomer to the party.

Spencer Tait stood in the doorway, surveying the room critically as if he wasn't at all sure he wanted to enter. With obvious reluctance he finally came in. Immediately a svelte blonde latched on to him.

Following Devon's curious look, Sally said, "Ah, Spence. You may have trouble with him."

"I already have." Devon's tone was terse, but she couldn't take her eyes off him.

"Well, he *did* idolize Jack Leif."

Devon was only half listening to Sally. The blonde was smiling adoringly at Tait. As she talked to him animatedly she occasionally touched his hand or shoulder.

"I think Jack was like a father to him. He gave Spence his start in the business years ago," Sally was saying.

Turning her attention back to Sally, Devon asked, "What else do you know about him?"

"It's hard to say. I've heard a lot of contradictory things about him. Some people hate him and others say he's the only man in town with integrity. I understand he was orphaned in Texas or some such place and made his way to LA. One thing's for sure: He's terribly attractive."

"You think so?"

"Definitely. Oh, he's not handsome in the usual pretty-boy way you usually find in Hollywood. And he isn't terribly tall—probably not much taller than you. But there's something about him. He has an air of quiet confidence. He doesn't have to brag; you just know that he's terrific in bed."

"Sally! You sound quite taken with the man."

"Oh, no. I don't want a one-night stand. And from what I hear, that's all you can expect from him."

"I'm surprised he's so popular, then, if that's his reputation."

"I think it's that air of mystery," Sally mused. "It's irresistible. Makes you want to try to figure him out. He's not part of the social scene, rarely goes to parties. But make no mistake: He's wired to all the power grids and grapevines. And he's the power behind the throne at UFS. I don't mean to tell you your job, but you'll have to get along with him."

"I know. But right now I'd rather not think about it."

Sally looked at her curiously. "He must've made you really mad."

"He did."

Just then a financial vice-president interrupted the conversation to ask Devon's views on coventure deals with other studios. Soon other executives joined the small group. Finally, realizing that she wouldn't get another opportunity to talk to Devon alone, Sally drifted off.

After an hour of shop talk Devon excused herself on the pretext of getting something to eat from the lavish buffet in the dining room. Actually she wasn't at all hungry, but felt the need for some breathing room. She was tired of being stared at, tired of being questioned in indirect ways about her plans for the studio.

She slipped through the French doors in the dining room and into the small private garden behind the bungalow. The air was cold and crisp, but she didn't mind. Her cashmere dress was warm, and the invigorating air made her mind feel clear again.

Now I know how monkeys at the zoo feel, Devon thought drily. Well, at least I saw Sally again. It's such a relief to see her looking happy. And it'll be fun to work together. . . .

A cough broke the stillness of the night as well as her thoughts, startling her. Whirling around, she saw Spencer Tait sitting on a bench only a few feet from her.

"Oh!" she said. Suddenly, after making conversation easily all evening, she couldn't think of a thing to say. She felt utterly stupid, and the "Oh!" seemed to hang like a visible object in the space between them. Mustering her composure, she reached for something to say.

"Sorry . . . I didn't mean to disturb you."

"You didn't," he replied evenly. "I just cleared my

throat to let you know you weren't alone. It seemed an unfair advantage for me to have. I could see you but you didn't know I was here."

Rising politely, he stood beside the bench.

"I'm sorry," Devon heard herself say again. She wished she'd just excused herself and returned to the party.

"It's okay. I'm just playing hookey for a while. Like you."

It had been all right until he added that *like you*.

"Well, I'll leave you alone. I just needed a breath of fresh air."

As she turned to go back into the bungalow, Tait insisted, "Please, don't go on my account." He took a large white handkerchief from his hip pocket. Whipping it open, he smiled. "Truce? Please sit down."

He spread the handkerchief on the bench. "Actually it's probably perfectly clean. After all, if you can't trust the Beverly Hills Hotel . . ."

Devon hesitated, unsure what to do. She really didn't want to go back inside. It was fatiguing to be stared at and questioned and fawned over. But neither did she want to stay out there, alone with Spencer Tait. She didn't want to risk continuing that morning's quarrel with him. His insulting accusation had tainted her entire day.

Motioning again to the empty space, he said invitingly, "Please sit down. I promise I won't bite. Besides, I was just sitting here, trying to figure out a way to speak to you alone."

It was amazing, Devon thought, how different he was this evening. That morning his voice had been angry and intimidating, his green eyes cold with fury. Now his voice was soft, almost seductive, with a hint of a Texas accent that Devon hadn't noticed earlier. And the expression in his eyes was warm and friendly.

Quickly she weighed her options. She could bid him a cool good evening and return to the party.

She could tell him exactly what she thought of him, releasing all the pent-up anger she still felt from their earlier encounter. Or she could simply sit down and listen to what he had to say. She knew she needed his support if she were to stay in her job. Harrison had made that clear.

As far back as high school Devon had been voted the most likely to succeed. Now she showed the astuteness that had won her that honor. She sat down. But she put as much distance between herself and Tait as possible.

"I've been watching you," he said evenly. "I'm impressed. Frankly I expected you to hang on to Harrison's arm all evening."

In spite of her resolve to be pleasant, Devon felt herself grow angry again. The man had an unerring ability to hit an exposed nerve every time they talked.

"I'm sure Harrison has no desire to run interference for me," Devon answered. "And besides, he'll be gone shortly. I've got to deal with these people on my own."

"You're not what they expected." Looking at her intently, he added, "Not what I expected either."

"I can't tell if that's meant to be a compliment or an insult."

Tait smiled, a soft, warm, engaging grin. To her chagrin Devon felt her guard relax, felt her tenseness melt away under the impact of that devastating smile. For the first time she felt Spencer Tait's potent charm. And she understood why so many women, apparently, had gladly taken what little he was willing to give them.

"It's meant to be a compliment," he finally replied, still watching her closely.

He was offering her an olive branch, Devon knew. Yet, she didn't know how to respond. She had managed to speak cordially, confidently, to everyone in the bungalow. Even to people whom she strongly suspected disliked or resented her. But she found it impossible to carry on a civil conversation with this man.

I can't make small talk with him, she decided. I've got to come right out with it.

Taking a deep breath, she said, "I didn't get this job by sleeping with Harrison."

"I know that now," Tait replied, meeting her direct look.

"Harrison hired me because he thinks I can do the job."

"I know that. I talked to Jack. He filled me in on the whole mess."

Devon ignored his reference to Leif. She wouldn't touch that with a ten-foot pole. She was going to have enough trouble with this man without becoming involved in an argument over his friend. Instead she said, "I can do this job. But you don't agree, do you?"

"No."

"Because I'm a woman?"

"Yes." Before Devon could protest angrily, he explained, "Believe it or not, I'm not a complete chauvinist. I was raised in a pretty traditional environment, I admit, where pink was for girls and blue for boys. But I've learned a few things since then. I don't think men are, by nature, better qualified to run studios or do any other job, for that matter. But there *are* certain harsh realities that work against women."

"That's an archaic point of view. Do you think women simply can't be tough enough to make unpopular decisions? Because if so, you're wrong. We can do what has to be done to be efficient and effective."

"But women tend to be more concerned with what people think of them. Men are conditioned to be harsh when necessary."

"As Harrison was with Jack Leif," Devon couldn't

resist pointing out. She regretted the words the moment they left her mouth.

He'll think I'm baiting him, she realized. Well, it's too late now to take back what I've said.

But to her surprise he didn't respond. Deciding she'd gone this far and might as well get it all said, she continued, "Harrison's first responsibility is to his company. He had to make a hard decision when it was called for. I would have done the same, even if I admired the person I was firing, even if it was a friend. Integrity doesn't have a gender, Mr. Tait."

He smiled. "Call me Spence. It looks like we'll be working together after all." He hesitated, then added pointedly, *"Boss."*

"So you'll keep an open mind about me?"

The smile left his face and he replied bluntly, "Even if you were the best-qualified woman in the world, you'd still have a harder time running this studio than the average equally qualified male. I'm sorry, but that's just the way it is."

"Are you so sure of that?"

"Listen, this town operates on rumor, innuendo, gossip. When the president of a studio or network has an affair, everyone talks about it. But it's accepted, almost expected. He's just doing what comes naturally in a town filled with gorgeous girls who will do anything to get ahead."

Devon knew how true that was. The "casting couch" wasn't an outdated cliché; it was still very much in evidence.

"The same rules and standards of behavior don't apply to women," Spence continued. "Your personal life is much more open to scrutiny and criticism than a man's would be. If you have an affair, it will be judged on the basis of how it might affect your job. There's a sexual double standard that will hurt you."

"I won't argue with you. But my personal life is *my* business and no one else's. I have no intention of letting it affect my job."

"You won't have any choice, Miss O'Neill. Half the executives at UFS will be eagerly waiting to watch you fail, and the other half will be actively working for it so they'll have a shot at your job. The first time there's the slightest hint of impropriety, you'll be judged harshly."

"I can handle that."

"Can you? I don't think any woman can."

Devon bristled. "I'm not *any* woman. I'm the president of this studio, and I intend to remain so. You're wrong in what you're saying. And I'll thoroughly enjoy proving it."

As she rose he looked at her with renewed respect. "I imagine you will, boss."

Without bothering to respond, she strode defiantly back into the bungalow.

Chapter 3

DEVON HURRIED UP THE BRICK WALK TO HER FRONT DOOR. Her house, located in Cheviot Hills, an older area of charming houses between Beverly Hills and West Los Angeles, was a pretty Cape Cod style. It had white shingles and clapboard siding and was trimmed in old brick. As she inserted the key in the door she thought of how her mother always referred to it as a "cottage." Compared to the house Devon had grown up in, it was just that. There was a large living room with a brick fireplace and a window seat in the big bay window. At one end of the living room was the dining area, with French doors leading into the garden.

Off to the other side were the bedrooms. The first Devon used as a study. The focal point of the room was her father's desk, handsomely carved of walnut and dating from the Civil War.

Next to the study was Devon's bedroom. It was the only area of the house she'd had remodeled. As she entered it now, tossing her camel-colored wool coat on a chair, she breathed a sigh of relief. The night was over. She felt much more peaceful just being home again.

She walked into the dressing room, with its cedar-lined wardrobes, and took out a nightgown. After quickly undressing, she slipped on a white silk Charmeuse gown with delicate French Alençon lace at the neck and wrists. Then she went into the large plant-filled bathroom and washed her face.

When she returned to the bedroom, she looked at it for just a moment before turning out the light. It was the retreat she'd asked the architect to make, with a wood-beamed ceiling and French doors. Beyond the doors was a redwood deck that encircled an old jacaranda tree. The room was furnished in light-colored country French furniture. The lime green of the silk comforter on the bed was repeated in the graceful, flowing lines of the oriental carpet on the gleaming hardwood floor.

For a moment Devon breathed in the peace and serenity of her home before flicking the switch and bathing the room in darkness.

It certainly wasn't the house she grew up in, she thought wryly. Sheila O'Neill was the epitome of a movie star, and her home was exactly what her fans expected her to have. It was certainly glamorous. Yet, what Devon remembered most about the southern Colonial-style mansion in the heart of Beverly Hills wasn't the staff of servants. Nor was it the priceless antiques, the Haviland china or the Waterford crystal sparkling on the massive dining room table that seated twenty.

What she remembered was the warmth that filled the house, the aura of love and security. It was a happy home, filled with laughter and pleasant conversation. Sheila and Justin O'Neill posed for magazine layouts in their formal rose garden, because it was all part of the image, the fantasy, that must be projected to maintain Sheila's career. But when the photographers were gone, they had picnics on the grass with Devon. And more often than not, they spent their evenings at home together.

Devon had tried to recapture some of that warmth in this house, though on a much smaller scale.

She opened a window to let fresh air fill the room while she slept. But when she lay down, she couldn't go to sleep.

As she looked out the open window at the stars blanketing the sky on that clear, cool night, she was reminded of something she'd read once. It had made a profound impression on her and she could still quote it word for word.

Tell me what you feel in your solitary room when the full moon is shining in upon you and your lamp is dying out, and I will tell you how old you are, and I shall know if you are happy.

Henri Frédéric Amiel had written that in his *Journal Intime*.

As the moon shone in upon Devon, her dark hair vivid against the white of the pillow, she thought about those words.

What do I feel in my solitary room? I feel a yearning. Not for Tony. I feel nothing for him any longer, not even bitterness. Even if he'd stayed with me, been faithful till the day he died, I would have been lonely with him. I would have realized that we weren't right for each other if I'd waited even six months, instead of marrying him so quickly.

Still, she admitted reluctantly to herself, it would be nice to have a warm body lying next to hers, someone who would look at her with love and understanding.

Since her divorce she had avoided getting too involved with anyone. She dated occasionally, mostly with men who were friends. It was safer that way. The divorce had hurt more than she'd let anyone know. When Tony had walked out, insisting their problems were *her* fault, Devon had known it wasn't true. It had just been his handy rationalization for moving on to someone else. If anything, she'd made a far stronger commitment to their marriage than he had.

And yet . . . there were times—in the middle of lonely nights or when she watched a mother hold a baby and wondered if she would ever experience that special fulfillment—when she wondered if he might be right. Had she sacrificed her personal life to her career? Was it possible to be open and vulnerable enough to know real intimacy and at the same time be tough enough to survive in a business that was male-dominated and ruthless?

Spencer Tait's words came back to haunt her. Was he right in suggesting that she couldn't be president of a studio and still have the luxury of falling in love if she chose?

When Harrison hired her, he had said, "I suppose you must feel like your ultimate fantasy has come true."

But the studio presidency was not quite that. Her most cherished fantasy had nothing to do with power and position. It was very, very different. It was inspired by a scene from *Gone With the Wind*. She'd first seen the movie as an impressionable thirteen-year-old, and she could still vividly remember sitting in the darkened theatre, watching an arrogant Rhett Butler carry a feebly protesting Scarlett O'Hara up a broad, curving staircase to their bedroom. The determined look in his eyes was a promise of secret delights and mysterious pleasures.

Devon had had no idea then what exactly went on behind bedroom doors. But she had known instinctively it was wonderful, and she had shivered with delicious expectation.

Even Tony, who was easily the sexiest man Devon had ever encountered, couldn't quite fulfill that expectation. Her ultimate fantasy was a man who could make her shiver as she had done once, long ago.

"Tell me what you feel in your solitary room . . ."

To Devon's surprise she suddenly realized she was thinking of emerald eyes that watched her with all the wariness and curiosity of a cat . . . and the man who, for the first time in a very long time, made her think about falling in love.

Chapter 4

Spence stood at the window in his bedroom, looking out at the black ocean that melted into the darkness. He was naked, his body lean and hard and tanned a golden honey color. On this still, cool night the waves he watched so intently were gentle, a low froth of silver on the empty beach.

I'd like to go for a swim right now, he thought, but I do have neighbors. Even at midnight some of them are still awake. And it isn't worth the bother of putting on swim trunks.

He felt restless. He wanted to do something, but he wasn't sure what. Earlier he'd thought he wanted to go to bed with Lisa Dowling, the blonde from the party, who'd made it clear she was available. But after getting back home and making love, he still felt dissatisfied somehow.

It wasn't Lisa's fault, he knew. She was attractive enough, with a body that she worked hard to keep in shape. She was as expert in bed as any thirtyish single woman whose sex life has been lustily uninhibited. But as he held her, touched her, lost himself in his naturally intense passion, he felt something was missing.

It was like every other time, and Lisa was like every other woman. There was nothing different, nothing special, nothing that touched his heart as well as his body.

You expect too much, he told himself, not for the first time. If it's love you want, go back to Tricia. She was great at saying all the right things with touching sincerity. Of course at the same time she was sleeping with each one of her leading men. Everyone in town knew it before I did. What was it Jack said about Tricia? "Easy it is of a cut loaf to steal a shive." Shakespeare. Jack was trying to get me to laugh at the situation so I wouldn't have to cry. Well, he's got his problems too. That latest wife of his . . . God, what fools men are over women. I was with Tricia. She was so beautiful. And smart. Smart enough to fool me.

Suddenly Lisa came out of the bathroom. She was wearing Spence's white terry robe. It was charmingly too big, the sleeves drooping past her fingers. Spence knew she was trying for the little-girl-lost effect. But somehow it came off a bit too calculated.

Walking up to him, she slipped her arms around his bare shoulders. Her big chocolate-brown eyes opened wide as she said, "Darling, you look positively morbid standing here in the dark. I'll turn on a light."

"No, I'll do it," he insisted, pulling away from her just a bit too eagerly.

He grabbed another robe out of his closet, then turned on a lamp.

Lisa looked at him shrewdly. He sensed that she realized innocence wasn't working and was now changing her approach.

Glancing around the large, surprisingly Spartan bedroom, she commented, "So this is how the other half lives."

He smiled slightly but said nothing.

"It isn't what I expected," she continued. "Where's your Oscar?"

"I thought it looked out of place somehow," he replied, not really answering her question. He wasn't about to explain to her that he had given it to his former teacher, Miss Ruth Ann Mayberry. Lisa simply wouldn't understand.

Miss Mayberry, as Spence still thought of her, had rescued him when he was drowning in a sea of loneliness and aimlessness. She was a dedicated teacher and a caring human being. In another time she would have been called a spinster. She was tall and spare, just like Katharine Hepburn in *The African Queen.* If she had had a love, he'd died in the Korean War. She had come to his high school the year he entered, the same year his mother died and his father started drinking.

He could still vividly remember her house. It had had books in every room and pots of green plants and interesting old furniture. She had served tea and hot chocolate in old, thin china and had told him he was important, that his life mattered. And for four years she had been his lifeline.

She had told him he was a good poet. She had convinced him he could be whatever he wanted to be. And when he had won the Oscar for Best Picture, he had sent it to her because she deserved it.

Looking at Lisa, Spence thought, she's nothing like Miss Mayberry. Not a companion, a soul mate. Just someone to spend a few hours with on a lonely night.

Suddenly it wasn't enough.

Sitting down in a chair by the telephone, he picked up the receiver. As he dialed he said to Lisa, "I'll call a cab."

Lisa looked startled, then angry. Obviously she'd expected to spend the night. But Spence had no desire to sleep with her, to hold her, to wake up beside her.

Though she looked like she wanted to say something bitchy, she didn't. She had known what to expect going in and had no right to complain.

"I'll get dressed, then," she finally said reluctantly. Grabbing the clothes she'd left in a pile on the floor, she went back into the bathroom, shutting the door just a little too loudly behind her.

Fifteen minutes later she was gone. And as far as Spence was concerned, it was as if she'd never been there.

In the living room he poured a stiff brandy from the bar, then took it back into the bedroom. Sitting down on the rumpled bed, he leaned against the oak headboard and slowly sipped the brandy. He'd already put Lisa out of his mind.

What he couldn't forget was the disturbing memory of his brief conversation with Devon O'Neill. Irritating woman, he thought, his mouth tightening into a frown.

But she did more than merely irritate him, he knew. She attracted him in some almost forgotten way. Something about her nudged at his memory . . . something about himself.

He turned off the light and tried to sleep. Count sheep, he told himself. He practiced deep breathing. Finally he sat on the edge of the bed and swore loudly. He shouldn't have sent Lisa home, he told himself. That had been stupid. She would have been happy to relax him. But some small voice deep inside told him that wouldn't have worked either. Devon O'Neill's presence was as strong as if she and not Lisa had been in the room with him.

"This is crazy!" he said aloud.

Grabbing a pair of jeans, he pulled them on and tugged a heavy pullover sweater over his head. He stepped out onto the deck off the bedroom, leaped down onto the beach and ran toward the hard sand where the waves washed and receeded.

When you can't beat 'em, join 'em, he told himself. All right, Miss Devon O'Neill, what is there about you that's keeping me awake? You're a beautiful woman, but I've seen many more beautiful in this town.

As he headed down the beach, racing with the waves, the sandpipers, and his thoughts, he tried to work out what was disturbing him. It wasn't just that she was the new president, that she had replaced his friend. Even Jack had admitted, "I did something wrong."

"Right," Spence had agreed. "First, your idea was stupid; second, you got caught. And rightly so."

That lady means to succeed, he thought now. She's determined to. And not because she needs to prove anything to *me*. She believes in herself. She's found her handle, her groove. . . .

Suddenly Spence stopped and threw back his head, laughing at the bright October moon. My God, that's it! She reminds me of Miss Mayberry.

And then he could see himself, a skinny, scared fourteen-year-old, listening to a handsome young woman say, " 'Every human being has some handle by which he may be lifted, some groove in which he was meant to run.' That's from Harriet Beecher Stowe's *Little Foxes*. Find your groove," Miss Mayberry had told him, "your own handle to the life you dream of."

Spence shoved his hands deep into the pockets of his jeans. He wished he'd asked Devon O'Neill if this was her dream or if she had just lucked out.

I'm as crazy as Jack, he thought. I send home a beautiful, willing blonde, then stand here in the moonlight, thinking about a stubborn brunette I've met twice and argued with both times.

Turning, he began to walk back toward his house. When he was almost at the deck, he stopped to watch the waves froth silver along the beach. He thought again of Devon. He saw her, not beautifully groomed in her stylish clothes, but rising from the waves, her hair a dark cloud about her beautiful face. He saw her slender, long-limbed, proud. Aphrodite.

Incongruously he remembered Lisa and her little-girl-lost routine. He'd bet that wouldn't be Devon O'Neill's style.

Shaking his head, he thought, Sorry, Lisa. You were outclassed tonight by a lady who's determined to prove me a liar.

For some inexplicable reason he laughed aloud, filled with a wonderful sense of exhilaration.

Chapter 5

THE NEXT MORNING AT NINE O'CLOCK DEVON SAT AT THE
head of the large table in the conference room next to
her office. She was dressed, as usual, with simplicity
and understated good taste. A white cashmere sweater
and matching cardigan over a white wool skirt con-
cealed the lush softness of her body. At this meeting
she was an executive first and a woman second.

Around her were the studio department heads—the
chief of worldwide production, executive vice-president
for marketing and the senior vice-presidents in charge
of physical production, business affairs, advertising,
administration, the television division and the cable
division.

With one exception, the head of the cable division,
they were all men.

As she looked at them Devon could almost hear what
they were thinking. Is she going to fire us and bring in
her own people? Will she shelve all the current projects
and replace them with her own?

And beneath the natural concern at the change in leadership was something more, something distinctly unsettling.

They don't want me to succeed, Devon suddenly realized. Reluctantly she faced the possibility that Tait had been right when he'd said most of these executives would like to see her fail.

It didn't entirely surprise her. And she couldn't let it bother her. She simply had to get on with her job to show these people that she was very definitely in charge and intended to remain so.

The night before, after the party, she'd studied the projects the studio had in development or production. Now, as she ran down the list of projects, she asked pointed questions of the people around her.

"*Domino*?"

"On schedule and under budget," Mark Tyson, the young head of worldwide production, responded crisply.

"*Dead Time*?" Devon continued.

"The advertising campaign is ready," the senior vice-president in charge of advertising answered. "Basically we're saying it's the new film by the master of suspense, Rod Cooper."

"Good." Devon nodded. "Why don't you screen it for me this evening? And bring the ad proofs along." Turning to Jed Munro, the eager young marketing vice-president, she asked, "How is it scheduled to open?"

"There's a premiere at the Bruin Theatre in Westwood, with the benefits going to the American Civil Liberties Union. The two leads have promised to show. Then it opens at Loews on the East Side of Manhattan. After three weeks it opens wide in about eight hundred theatres."

"Why aren't you opening it wide immediately?"

"Because the subject matter's so political and not

automatically appealing to a mass audience. We wanted time to build word of mouth and get good reviews. Jack thought . . ." Munro stopped and looked distinctly uncomfortable.

"It's all right," Devon assured him calmly. "Jack Leif's name *can* be mentioned." Then she continued, "Is the film that good?"

"We previewed it for the critics and the studio employees Friday night and they seemed to love it. I talked to a critic from the LA *Times* and she was crazy about it."

"Okay, that sounds fine. But in the future I don't want to focus exclusively on the LA and New York markets. Not that they're unimportant, especially in terms of publicity. But there *are* a lot more people in the rest of the country."

She paused, then added, "You know, not everyone reads the reviews of the New York critics. Most people decide for themselves which films to see."

"I don't even understand those critics half the time," Tyson responded, grinning impudently.

Everyone laughed, and for the first time the tension that had filled the room from the beginning of the meeting seemed to dissipate. Devon flashed Tyson a disarming smile. She wanted to get along with these people so that working together would be a pleasure. Though she was prepared to be tough if she had to be, she preferred a working atmosphere that was congenial and not fraught with dissension and political infighting.

"Now, on to *Love Affair,*" Devon continued, glancing down at her agenda.

"Looks great," Tyson answered confidently. "We have control of both the hardcover and paperback tie-ins. Shooting starts next week, and if everything goes well, the picture will open next June, along with the publication of the hardcover book."

"Things had better go well," Devon responded firmly. "As I understand it, we paid half a million for the movie rights to a first novel that was still in galleys."

Tyson looked uncomfortable but said nothing.

"What about *Charlie's Boys*?"

"A new writer's doing a fix," Tyson answered.

"Haven't there been two writers on it already?"

"Yes."

"What's the problem?" Devon pressed an obviously reluctant Tyson to elaborate.

"Well, it's Spence's production and he isn't satisfied with the scripts he's seen so far."

Devon hesitated. She knew Spencer Tait was bound to enter the conversation sooner or later, but she had hoped there would be no problems connected with him. She realized that everyone was watching her intently. Tait had too much power for her to treat him as firmly as she might treat others. His movies were a major source of revenue for the studio. On the other hand *she* was running the studio, and somehow she would have to make that clear.

Turning to Charles Woods, the vice-president in charge of business affairs, she asked, "What is our contract with Tait on this project?"

Woods was a tense-looking man in his late forties. He answered carefully, "Aside from money for the script, it's basically a back-end deal. No money up front. Frankly Jack wasn't crazy about this project, but Spence really wants to do it. In return for no front money Spence is being charged a low distribution fee."

"How low?"

"Below twenty-five percent. And the fee is tied to box-office grosses. If the movie does well, the fee will be even lower. If it does badly, the fee will escalate."

"How is Tait financing the production if we're not doing it?"

"If we like the final script, we'll provide the financing. If we don't, and if he can get financing elsewhere, we'll still distribute it."

"So right now we're only committed to pay for the script?" Devon asked.

"Exactly."

"Obviously Mr. Tait is taking full advantage of that by hiring as many writers as he sees fit. Tell him that if he can't find the right writer for this project, that's *his* problem. We won't pay for any more rewrites after this one." She finished pointedly, "And tell him if he has any questions about this policy to bring them to me directly."

Woods looked as if he didn't relish the prospect of telling Spencer Tait anything of the sort. After a long pause he cleared his throat nervously, then replied, "I'll tell him."

"Okay. Now on to *Buddies*."

"It's way over budget," Tyson admitted reluctantly.

"Don't we have a contractual clause penalizing the director for exceeding the budget?" Devon asked.

"Yes," Woods answered.

"But you know Hanson," Tyson chimed in. "He's difficult to control. He's obsessive about every shot being absolutely perfect. But the dailies look fantastic. We've got a potential Oscar-nominee there."

After a thoughtful pause Devon replied, "I'll go along with it because it's Hanson and his track record is impeccable. But I'm going to have a talk with him. And as a general rule, from now on we don't work with people who are known to cause this kind of problem. Wasting money simply to satisfy an inflated ego is pointless. There are many good young directors, eager for a chance, who'd bring the project in under budget."

"There's going to be a single from the movie," Munro interjected.

"Good. Make sure it's released before the movie

comes out to build awareness of the movie." She continued, "Now, what about *Jacks*?"

It was Spencer Tait's latest film, and she knew it was doing extremely well at the box office.

"It's grossed over a hundred million," Tyson responded. "Next month it will have a royal premiere in London."

"Good." Devon closed her notebook and leaned back in her chair. "I think that's all for now. I want to finish by saying I look forward to working with all of you."

She was pleased to see that her calculated reassurance seemed to relax everyone. They left looking less worried than when they'd come in.

Devon immediately called Sally's office, which was in another part of the building.

"I'll be right there," Sally said eagerly.

When Devon hung up, Marci buzzed her on the intercom.

"Yes, Marci?"

"Some flowers just came for you, Miss O'Neill."

"Flowers? Is there a card?"

"Yes. Do you want me to read it?"

"No, just bring the flowers in here."

A moment later Marci came in carrying a magnificent bouquet of yellow roses. She set them on a corner of Devon's desk, then waited expectantly.

Devon knew Marci was curious about the sender. She was more than a bit curious herself, but she waited until Marci had left before she opened the envelope. Taking out the white card, she silently read:

"With profound apologies for my inexcusable behavior."

It was signed, "The cretin."

"Just what are you smiling about so slyly?" Sally asked from the open doorway.

Startled, Devon looked up. She hadn't been aware

she was smiling. "Oh, nothing," she answered evasively.

"Three dozen yellow roses aren't what I would call nothing."

"Let's get some lunch; I'm starving," Devon said quickly, changing the subject. But as she left she carefully placed the card in her desk drawer instead of tossing it in the wastepaper basket.

"I brought the *Last Chance* script," Sally said, holding up a thick white manuscript.

"Good." Turning to Marci, Devon explained, "I'll be at the commissary for about an hour."

As she and Sally walked out together, she told herself she was relieved at Spence's gesture for purely professional reasons. After all, they had to work together, and this would make that easier to do.

But secretly she was charmed by the man.

Late that night Devon lay in bed, reading the script of *Last Chance*. It was everything Sally had said and more. It had adventure, romance, pathos and humor. Devon had been too young to see the original when it was first released, but she'd seen it on television some years earlier and enjoyed it immensely. This version, she suspected, would be even better because it wouldn't be limited to a sound stage. The writer-director's descriptions of the scenes as he envisioned them sounded magnificent.

The story opens with a newly widowed woman determined to bring her teen-age daughter out west to some land her late husband had been homesteading. They are guided by a disreputable yet engaging mountain man, whom the woman eventually falls in love with. Along the way they pick up a teen-age boy, orphaned and on his own, imbued with an unrealistic sense of the "romance" of the West. Much of the story takes place during a treacherous winter crossing of the

Rockies. The themes are compelling and simple—love and survival. At the end the fiercely independent mountain man has allowed himself to become close to the woman. The boy has become a man and claims the daughter's love.

Closing the bound copy, Devon leaned back against the pillows thoughtfully. It was an excellent script. Karl Kreiss was a new young director whose rise was meteoric. His first two films were financial and critical successes. If they could get the right cast . . .

Devon felt a growing sense of excitement. This was good enough to warrant being her first project at UFS. Though she was already responsible for the projects in progress at the studio, they weren't really *hers*. Other people had chosen them, cast them, guided them. This would be hers from the very beginning. She would nurture it, shape it, watch it grow.

With a self-effacing smile, she reminded herself that she would have to take responsibility for its failure if that should happen. But she didn't think it would. She had a firm conviction that this was something that could be very big indeed.

Putting the script on her bedside table, she turned off the light and tried to go to sleep. But her mind was working furiously, considering possible actors, possible locations. She didn't fall asleep until hours later.

The next morning she called Sally into her office. Not wanting to put Sally through one more minute of uncertainty, she came straight to the point. "I love it. Let's make a picture."

Sally's face broke into a huge grin. "Oh, Dev, I knew you'd like it!"

"Let's see if we can structure a deal with Kreiss and then get him to come in for a meeting."

"I happen to know he's very anxious to do this film," Sally said enthusiastically.

Pressing the intercom, Devon consulted Marci about a good time for a meeting.

"You're free from three o'clock to four," Marci answered after a pause to check the appointment calendar.

"Ask Kreiss to come in then," Devon said to Sally. "In the meantime I'll tell Charlie Woods to contact his agent and start the deal-making. And another thing, Sally: I want *you* to produce this."

Sally didn't look entirely surprised, and Devon realized she'd been hoping that would happen.

"I appreciate the vote of confidence, Dev. I won't let you down."

"I know you won't. Besides, that's what the Old Girls' Network is all about—helping each other. You brought this project to me. You believed in it when no one else did. I couldn't turn it over to someone else who might not have the same degree of commitment to it. Can you work with Kreiss?"

"Oh, yes!" Sally answered quickly. She blushed, then looked away nervously.

Devon had the feeling that there was something left unsaid. But when Sally remained silent, she continued, "I don't think the script needs rewriting. So let's start thinking about casting. We'll draw up a list when we meet this afternoon."

"Were you thinking of shooting this winter? If so, that only gives us two or three months for preproduction."

"Yes. I know it's rushing things, but if we don't do it now, we'll have to wait until next November or December, when there's snow again. And I don't want to wait that long. Do you think you and Kreiss could be ready to shoot that quickly?"

"Definitely!" Sally answered without hesitation. Then she added, "Oh, Dev, you don't know what this means to me. When Jerry left, everything seemed so awful, and now . . ."

Her voice trailed off helplessly. For a moment Devon felt ill at ease. As she looked at Sally she thought how fragile she was, how terribly vulnerable emotionally. In an odd way she thought, fate hadn't been kind in making Sally so lovely. If she'd been plain but still brilliant, perhaps she would have been able to concentrate more on her work and wouldn't have needed so much from men. As it was, she felt that without a man she was a failure, no matter how well her career was going.

But am I so different? Devon asked herself. I told myself my career filled the void when Tony left. But it didn't completely. . . . No, not completely.

However, that was something she didn't want to think about just then.

Sally's extremely capable, she told herself. There's no reason why she can't do this job.

To Sally she said, "I'll see you this afternoon, then."

"Great!" Sally responded with a brilliant smile, then left.

As Devon sat at the desk, she had to admit there was one serious problem with the project. Leif was right about the cost. It could be astronomical. But with carefully structured deals, they might keep the cost down to around twenty million dollars and still afford "bankable" stars.

If the film did get out of control financially, and especially if it failed at the box office, Devon knew she would be the first casualty.

We need a coventure partner, she thought. That will spread the risk. And if the picture's as successful as I think it can be, there would still be enough profits to go around.

She considered the possibilities. She could approach

Chase Manhattan Bank for a production loan. They were one of the few banks in film financing, and normally they required only foreign contracts as collateral. There were also private investors, as well as other studios.

Suddenly she had an idea. Her blue eyes sparkled and her lips parted slightly in a sly grin. She knew exactly who she wanted as a partner—Spencer Tait. This would cement her business relationship with him, a necessity if she wanted to remain at the studio for long. And, much as she told herself the man irritated her, she had to admit his pictures were excellent. The more she thought about it, the more she realized he was the best person to be the executive producer on this film. He would make it a quality picture.

Buzzing Marci, Devon asked her to get Spence on the phone. Less than a minute later Marci told her he was holding for her.

Picking up the telephone, Devon said pleasantly, "Good morning."

"Good morning. What can I do for you?"

"I have a property that I think would be an excellent coventure for the studio and your company."

"Oh?" His tone was carefully neutral, yet Devon clearly detected a note of curiosity. She knew he must be surprised at her offer. He had never done a coventure before.

She explained, "It's a terrific story, but it's wall-to-wall location, and I'm afraid it could get expensive. I'd like to discuss it with you in person."

"Why me? Why not another studio?" he asked pointedly. "I've never done this before. Usually I come to you guys for money."

"Yes, but you've got a lot of cash right now from *Jacks*. So I figure you can afford a coventure. And I want someone with your high standards, and your track record, to make this picture."

"In other words you're not taking any chances with the first movie you're doing here," Spence commented frankly.

"Exactly. Are you interested?"

There was a pause. Through the telephone Devon could sense Spence's mind racing, considering the pros and cons of her offer. Would he do it? she wondered.

Finally he said, "Send the script over. I'll take a look at it and see if I'm interested."

Devon breathed a sigh of relief. "Perhaps we could have a meeting tomorrow?" she suggested.

"I'm going out of town for a week. I'm leaving early in the morning."

"Oh." Devon was disappointed. She didn't want to wait a week to find out if Spence was interested. If he wasn't, she would have wasted a lot of valuable time when she could have been looking for another coventure partner.

"Well," she continued, "perhaps we could meet this afternoon. . . ."

"No, I'll need a few hours to read the script and think about it. I have an idea. We'll talk about it over . . ." he paused, then finished drily, "a *relationship* dinner."

Devon couldn't help laughing. She knew exactly what he meant. In Hollywood one had to do business with all sorts of people, including people one didn't like, because the community was so small. Therefore, people often had "relationship" meetings—in restaurants, at their beach houses on weekends—not because they enjoyed each other's company, but because they wanted to cement a good business relationship.

"All right," she agreed. "Why don't we meet for drinks first at the Polo Lounge."

"That isn't my style. There's a little Italian restaurant I know of. Why don't I pick you up about eight and we'll go there."

Devon hesitated. This sounded more like a date than

she would have liked. But she had no choice. "Okay," she finally agreed.

"Where do you live?"

"In Cheviot Hills. One-eleven Martindale Drive."

"I'll see you then. 'Bye."

After hanging up, Devon sat quietly for a moment. The day before, she wouldn't have dreamed she would be having dinner alone with Spencer Tait. That night, that was just what she would be doing.

Well, she thought dryly, it should certainly be interesting.

Chapter 6

AT A QUARTER TO EIGHT THAT NIGHT DEVON SAT AT THE glass-topped vanity table in her bedroom, applying makeup. She had dressed in a fluid jersey blouse and skirt in a deep shade of berry that went well with her dark complexion. The blouse was actually a combination blouse-jacket. The bodice was quilted with jet trim, and the sleeves were long and sheer. The slim, hip-hugging skirt barely covered her knees.

She pulled her hair back from one side of her face with an ivory comb and let the rest fall in thick waves around her other cheek. As always she wore little jewelry, only pearls at her ears. Her makeup was equally simple—sheer lip gloss, a light dusting of blush across her cheekbones, silver-blue shadow on her eyelids, and a touch of mascara on her naturally dark lashes.

If she looked decidedly less businesslike and much more feminine tonight, it wasn't a choice she had made consciously. But she *was* conscious of a barely suppressed tingle of excitement.

From the vanity she picked up a crystal atomizer made by Marcel Franck of Paris nearly a hundred years before. As she sprayed the musky scent behind her ears and in her cleavage, she wondered what the other women who had used the atomizer had thought as they prepared to go out. Did the *Belle Époque* beauty hope the seductive scent would drive her lover to propose? Did the free-spirited flapper merely hope it would lead to an uninhibited interlude in a rumble seat?

But I'm not meeting my lover, Devon reminded herself abruptly. This is a business meeting.

Sure, a tiny voice deep inside mimicked snidely.

The doorbell rang promptly at eight, as if on cue. Devon grabbed her slim evening bag and a sequined shawl before answering the door. She had no intention of inviting Spence inside.

He was dressed casually, as usual, in a red V-neck cashmere pullover that revealed his muscular, tanned chest. The matching ivory slacks fit his flat stomach and hard thighs smoothly. Not for the first time Devon reflected that Spence was different from the men she was used to meeting in the business. He didn't look or act "Hollywood." There was simply nothing phony about him. He was very much his own man. Sure of himself, he didn't try to impress. He wasn't constantly "on," as were so many people.

Devon found that tremendously refreshing and, on a very profound level, a bit unsettling. She didn't know what to expect from him, couldn't anticipate his moves.

"I see you're ready," he said with a smile.

"I didn't want to keep you waiting. We have a great deal of business to discuss."

"Okay. Let's go."

They drove down Motor Avenue, a broad street bordered on the north end by Twentieth Century–Fox studios, and on the south by the high, French-vanilla-colored walls of Metro-Goldwyn-Mayer. Then they turned onto the Santa Monica Freeway and five minutes later were merging onto the Pacific Coast Highway. Spence's maroon Jaguar sedan was quiet and comfortable. But somehow Devon had expected him to own something more flashy. A Ferrari or a Rolls would have been more typical of a successful producer.

No, she thought again, he doesn't feel the need to impress. He must be very secure, indeed.

"Did you like the script?" she asked, determined to focus on business.

"Yes. Very much. But I can see why you're worried about the budget. This could be an extremely expensive failure. The film business has seen too many big budget flops the past couple of years."

"It could be, but it won't. Most big budget failures happen because the story is too weak to warrant so much money being spent on it. And the studios don't maintain careful control of the production. I intend to watch *Last Chance* closely. And you just said you like the story. If we're careful, I think this could be very profitable."

"I like the fact that it appeals to a twofold audience, the young and the old," Spence replied. "That's a nice change. What do you see as the budget?"

"Well, of course that will depend on the cast, but I think it can be kept below twenty million."

Spence raised one blond eyebrow quizzically. "Isn't that a bit optimistic?"

"Not if there isn't any skimming off the top," Devon answered. Her tone was blunt, her gaze direct.

Spence laughed. It was an uninhibited, full-throated sound that was very pleasant.

"You mean, if I do this with UFS, you don't expect me to build a screening room onto my house and charge it to the production?"

Grinning, she answered, "If I thought you'd do that, I wouldn't have approached you in the first place."

"I see." After a moment he said thoughtfully, "You know, when I first started in the business, I heard a very successful producer say he only made big-budget pictures because you can't steal a million dollars from a two-million-dollar picture. I thought he was kidding. Later I realized he wasn't."

There was no need to reply to this, Devon knew. She was as aware as Spence was of the extent of "creative bookkeeping" in Hollywood. It was the reason most big stars insisted on getting their money up front, in multimillion-dollar salaries, rather than taking "points," or a percentage of the profits.

Soon they arrived at the restaurant, a small, cozy place on the Malibu Pier. The owner knew Spence well and greeted him warmly. With an admiring glance at Devon he said to Spence, "For you the very best table." He led them to a table for two near a cheerfully blazing fireplace.

After they ordered, Devon began to talk about the project again, but Spence stopped her.

"There's something I want to say before we go any further. I want to apologize for my behavior yesterday."

"Please . . . let's forget it. The roses are beautiful." She laughed softly. "And I loved the card."

He laughed too. Then he sobered and continued, "But you must let me tell you why I was such an ass. Jack is my friend. I owe him a lot. I respected him more than I respect anyone else in the business. When Harrison told me what had happened, I couldn't— wouldn't—believe it. So I took out my anger and disappointment with Jack on you."

"Are you sure it isn't more than that? Doesn't the fact that I'm a woman enter into it?"

Devon looked directly at him as she asked the

question. It was crucial to her that they be candid with each other. Game-playing took too much time, energy and, in this business, money.

He returned her look. For a moment each took the other's measure.

On the periphery of her vision Devon saw the candlelight flickering in the hurricane lamps, the diners at the adjoining tables, the waiters carrying trays of steaming food.

This is a moment of truth, she thought. This will determine whether or not we can work together.

Suddenly Spence smiled. Watching him, Devon felt her heart race and a flush suffuse her cheeks. His smile was absolutely dazzling.

"I have to admit I tend to have a pretty traditional viewpoint. As I told you before, I think women face special problems in this business, especially when they reach your level. But after I found out a bit more about you, I decided Harrison made a shrewd choice in picking you for the job."

Devon breathed an inward sigh of relief, though outwardly her expression was noncommittal. "On that positive note, let's stop talking about the past and think about the future. Will you work with me on this film?"

Spence was silent for a long moment. Finally he said slowly, "Yes. But on these conditions: Everything must be split equally—cable rights, cassettes, foreign rights —and I want an equal say in determining the number of prints to be made, the theatres the movie will be shown in, the advertising strategy and the budget."

"In short you want equality," Devon answered. "I can appreciate that. Agreed."

Spence smiled at the thinly disguised barb. Then he continued, "There's one more thing. And it's crucial, a deal-breaker."

"Yes?"

"My company isn't big enough to absorb a big loss.

And despite your good intentions, this is the kind of picture that could very easily get out of hand. I want a clause in the contract that stipulates that if the picture goes more than ten percent over budget, I can back out and take my financing with me."

Devon hesitated. She wasn't seriously concerned about the picture going over budget. She had tremendous confidence in Sally's ability to handle the production. And she intended to watch it carefully. And yet . . . if somehow something did go wrong, it would put UFS in an untenable position. The studio would have to finish the picture on its own or declare the project, and all the money spent on it, a loss.

The more she thought about Spence's condition, the less acceptable it appeared.

"Do you realize the position you're putting me in if I agree to that clause?" Her voice was well in control, but there were silvery sparks in her blue eyes.

"Yes. And I realize the position you'll be putting me in if I don't insist on it and something goes wrong." His attitude was unyielding, his tone truculent.

Before Devon could respond, he added, "You're playing hardball now, lady. I'm willing to risk my own ten million dollars. What are you willing to risk?"

Blue eyes met green ones defiantly. This was exactly the sort of challenge that brought out Devon's "fighting Irish" heritage. Her decision about Spence's condition depended on her confidence in her own ability to handle a project of such magnitude.

If I can't handle it, then I have no business being in this position in the first place, she told herself.

Looking levelly at Spence, she said, "Okay. Our lawyers can draw up a deal memo as soon as I talk to Harrison and get his okay."

An agreement should have ended the flare-up. But they continued to look defiantly at one another for several long seconds. The tension was broken only when the waiter brought bowls of thick, steaming minestrone.

As she concentrated on eating for the next few minutes, Devon realized that what was sparking their anger was resentment. She resented Spence's influence at the studio and therefore over her, while he resented having a boss who not only had replaced his friend but was a woman.

When the waiter took their empty bowls away, Devon said to Spence, "Why don't you give me the benefit of the doubt and stop assuming I'm going for your jugular?"

Spence hesitated, then that dazzling smile softened his face. "If you agree to do the same. Now, about possible casting . . ."

For several minutes they discussed actors and actresses, and Devon was relieved to find that Spence's thinking mirrored her own. They had no disagreements in that crucial area. And although he was less impressed with Kreiss than she was, he agreed the man had done a good job writing the script and would probably be the best director for the project.

Then Devon mentioned that she had offered Sally the job of producer.

"She isn't experienced enough," Spence said flatly, in a tone that brooked no discussion.

But Devon wasn't about to give in on this crucial point. "Neither were you when you produced your first movie," she shot back. Once more her defiance made the tension between them so palpable that she felt she could almost touch it. "And I understand it grossed thirty million on a budget of half a million."

"I worked as an assistant producer for years before I got that chance!"

"Well, Sally's worked for years too. She's a production vice-president and she didn't get there by being incompetent."

"She's done nothing to prove she can handle a project this big. Hell, start her out on something small and see how she does before handing her a big-budget movie."

"You wouldn't ask her to prove herself if she were a man. That's the problem, isn't it?" Devon glared at Spence, who glared back.

"That *isn't* the problem, so don't try to use it as a convenient sidetrack."

"Then what exactly *is* the problem?" Devon asked in a tone that was dripping with sarcasm. "She was the only person at UFS who had enough sense to recognize a terrific script when she saw it. If it weren't for her, we wouldn't be doing this project in the first place. She deserves a shot at producing it."

Spence retreated into a stony silence for a moment. Finally he said, "Handing her this job is taking just too big a risk."

That cuts it, Devon thought furiously. She had no intention of letting Spencer Tait lecture her on the risk factor in making movies.

"I know as much about risk as you do. I know that in this business, decisions are made as much on the roll of the dice as anything else. Well, I've backed up this decision with sound reasons why Sally should have the job. You say she's too inexperienced, but the fact is she's had plenty of experience and deserves a shot at doing more."

Then, in a calculatedly even voice, Devon got to the heart of the argument. "If anyone's taking a risk by hiring Sally, it's *me*. With that clause you're insisting on, you've eliminated the risk for yourself. You can back out if it looks like it's too big a risk for you to handle. I can't without losing my job."

The challenge to Spence's ego worked. Devon knew he wasn't about to let her question his courage.

The tension that had suddenly come between them

evaporated just as quickly. "Okay," Spence agreed reluctantly. "I just hope your confidence in her is justified."

"It is," Devon said with quiet confidence as the waiter brought plates of scampi and lasagne.

As they ate they said nothing. But the silence was a comfortable one. The argument had been resolved. Both had won and lost in various ways. Neither wanted to dwell on the hard decisions that had finally been made.

Devon had intended to be cordial but impersonal with Spence that night. But she found herself increasingly intrigued by him. She had enjoyed the parry and thrust of their discussions of the film. In a way she had even enjoyed their disagreements. They were both people of strong convictions and high standards, determined to make the best possible films. Even while she was angry at him, she respected him.

Though he was in some ways as hard and arrogant as she expected a man in his position to be, in other ways he was surprisingly self-effacing. He had a healthy ego and the courage of his convictions. But his ego was well in hand; it didn't control him. And though he admittedly had certain prejudices about women, he was capable of overcoming them.

He reminded her of something her mother had once said about Spencer Tracy, who might have been his namesake. "He was secure enough to match wits with Kate Hepburn, who was as intelligent and witty as he."

Spence seemed to enjoy matching wits with her. She sensed he found their arguments as stimulating as she did.

Despite herself, she found herself wanting to know more about this fascinating man. Trying not to sound as if she were prying, she asked casually, "How did you get into the business in the first place?"

"I left home at eighteen and headed west. LA was as

far as I could go without getting wet. The only job anyone was willing to offer me was in the mailroom of a production company. The rest, as they say, is history."

Beneath the wry humor Devon sensed something much more serious. Though he was making light of it, it was clearly a painful subject for him, one he wouldn't discuss readily.

As they talked she discovered that he didn't like to discuss his early life. He'd obviously had a rough time of it. He knew surprising things about everything from bare-knuckle boxing to the safest way to hop a freight. But he didn't say a word about his childhood or his family.

Finally Devon hazarded a personal question. "Where are you from?"

He hesitated, then answered, "Galveston."

"That's a beautiful city. I was there once with my mother when she was on a promotional tour. I was impressed with it."

"I don't think you saw the part I come from," Spence replied dryly. Then, clearly wanting to change the subject, he added, "Your mother's Sheila O'Neill, isn't she?"

Now it was Devon's turn to pull back. She didn't like discussing her mother with people she didn't know well. The question was always the same: "Is she still as beautiful as ever?"

Now, Devon answered Spence's question tersely, "Yes, she's my mother."

To her surprise he didn't follow up with the usual questions. Instead he said, "Why didn't you become an actress? You have the looks and the connections."

Devon felt both surprised and flattered. Finally, after a slight pause, she answered, "I never had the slightest desire to follow in my mother's footsteps. Watching what she went through was enough to turn me off to that side of the business. She lived in a fishbowl. No privacy at all. I hated that."

"Yes," Spence agreed. "I can see how you would. That's why I've always kept a low profile. I can't stand being stared at when I walk down the street or being pestered by reporters who want to know who I'm sleeping with. It's none of their damn business."

"You don't want the notoriety. You just want the power," Devon said with sudden insight.

"Exactly," he said with a grin.

"Why? Is it the pleasures that go along with the power—money, sex, limousines at your beck and call? Or is it the ego trip of creating American popular culture?"

"I just want to have fun. Making movies is the most fun I've run across." Turning the tables, he said, "What about you, Miss O'Neill? What drives you?"

"I think it's time you called me Devon. And I just want to have fun too. I hated many of the side effects of my mother's career—the publicity, the narrow-minded people who wouldn't let her grow as an artist. But I loved the movies she made. My happiest moments as a child were sitting in a dark theatre, pretending that what was on the screen was real. I knew it was fantasy, but that didn't matter. It was all so much fun, watching fantasies come to life."

Spence looked at her soberly for a long moment. The piercing gaze from those green eyes was unnerving. Suddenly Devon felt as if her slip was showing or her lipstick was smeared.

She couldn't handle that kind of intense scrutiny from this disturbing man. She moved quickly to steer the tone of the conversation onto safer ground. When she asked Spence about his own background, immediately the atmosphere changed. Clearly Spence was reluctant to discuss his past.

"I didn't grow up rich the way you did," he said.

Devon reacted angrily to the barbed remark. "That didn't make me any less ambitious than you."

He smiled and his defensiveness seemed to melt away. "You're right. And I like that about you."

As they talked further Devon realized that Spence was very private about his emotions. Behind his independent, self-sufficient facade was an extremely sensitive man.

But I should have known that from his films, Devon thought. Only someone who feels deeply about things, who cares about people, could have made those pictures. He is far from being the cretin I called him.

She looked out the window at the Pacific Ocean glistening silver and ebony under the pale orange glow of a full moon. She realized that she was dangerously attracted to this man. She hadn't expected it and wasn't prepared for it.

The waiter came to clear away their plates, then asked if they cared for dessert. Spence ordered spumoni and coffee for both of them. "You're not one of those constant calorie counters, are you?" he asked with a disarming smile.

Devon shook her head. She sensed that he was biding his time, waiting to talk further when they would be free of interruptions. She liked that. Too many of the men she knew were quick, glib. Her father used to say, "Glibness is a prevalent disease in Hollywood. One that can destroy a career. It doesn't do any good for an agent to 'sell' an actor if the camera can't pick up something real in him."

So Devon waited now, comfortable that this man, at least, was attempting to be honest with her.

After the waiter had served the dessert and coffee, Spence looked at her. "What do you know about Harriet Beecher Stowe?" he asked.

"I beg your pardon?"

"Harriet Beecher Stowe. What does that name mean to you?"

"Well, Little Eva and Topsy. Simon Legree." She smiled. "Do you think I'm a villain, trying to start a civil war in Hollywood, female against male? Because I won't, you know."

"I know." A smile was playing about his lips, warming his eyes. He picked up his coffee, holding the cup in both hands as if warming himself. "I haven't told this to many people. In fact I'm not sure I've ever told it to anyone."

Devon waited, her curiosity piqued.

"There was a very special lady in my life—besides my mother, who died when I was fourteen. This lady, Ruth Ann Mayberry, was my teacher in high school. She introduced me to things I'd never heard of before, made me aware that I had options, that Galveston was only one small spot in a big world. She told me about Harriet Beecher Stowe."

He quoted the passage from *The Little Foxes*, then added, "She would look at us kids and paraphrase, 'Find *your* groove, your own handle to the life you dream of.' I just want you to know that I understand you're trying to find yours against a lot of resistance. And I admire you."

Devon felt a terribly strong yearning to reach across the table and touch those hands that were gripping the cup so tightly. But she resisted; instead she clasped her hands in her lap. However, she couldn't keep her respect—and something more, she knew—from showing in her eyes.

For a long moment green eyes held blue ones. Devon felt a quick flow of warmth, a quickening of desire.

Then the waiter returned to ask if they required anything more.

Spence never broke their gaze as he replied, "No, thank you. We're just fine."

But the moment was gone. Devon had remembered that she was this man's boss and couldn't, under any circumstances, give in to the growing attraction she felt for him.

Recognizing her withdrawal, Spence asked the waiter for the bill. Then they made their way out of the restaurant.

When he walked her up the brick path to her front door, he looked at her silently.

Searching for something to say, she finally commented, "That was a surprising quote from Harriet Beecher Stowe."

"She wrote something else you might find interesting," he replied. "It's about fantasies."

He quoted in that low, resonant voice, with its caress of southern accent:

> *It lives around us like a cloud,*
> *A world we do not see;*
> *Yet the sweet closing of an eye*
> *May bring us there to be.*

Intuitively Devon realized she was being offered a rare insight into Spencer Tait, this very private man.

"I think I know what makes you so successful at what you do," she said softly, her eyes meeting his unflinchingly. "You're in tune with your fantasies. You bring them to life."

"And what about you? What are your fantasies?"

Devon's voice caught in her throat, and for a moment she couldn't speak. Finally she responded in a voice that was barely more than a whisper, "I'm grown-up now. I'm not a child sitting in a darkened theatre, pretending that what I see is real. I don't have any fantasies."

Spence shook his head slowly in disagreement. "You

wouldn't be in this business if you didn't have some
fantasies still."

For an instant Devon hesitated, staring into his green
eyes as if mesmerized. Suddenly, unexpectedly, Spencer Tait had triggered in her romantic fantasies that she
had thought were gone with her failed marriage.

Almost immediately she realized just how thin was
the ice she was skating on. Spencer Tait was an
important business associate. She couldn't allow herself
to be intrigued by him.

"Good night," she said abruptly, anxious to escape
his too-perceptive gaze.

He understood. "Good night, boss," he said without
rancor.

Then he turned and strode back to his car.

As Devon entered her house, locking the door
securely behind her, she heard his car pull away.

Chapter 7

IN THE MIDDLE OF DEVON'S SECOND WEEK AS PRESIDENT of United Film Studios, her mother came to have lunch with her at the commissary. Though Sheila O'Neill hadn't made a movie in twenty years and no longer considered herself a movie star, there was something about her, as she swept into Devon's office, that belied those facts. Marci stared open-mouthed at her before finally finding the presence of mind to buzz Devon and announce Sheila's arrival.

She was fifty-six but looked at least ten years younger. Her dark hair had only a few attractive wisps of gray, and her face was nearly unlined. Her blue eyes sparkled with all the bright promise they had shown on the screen, and her figure was one a twenty-year-old would envy. Aside from being firmly committed to eating health food, she made no effort to maintain her beauty.

Hers was a radiance that came from within as well as without. She was an essentially happy person, with a generosity of spirit that few people, especially in Hollywood, could match. This had surprised more than one person meeting her for the first time. It was the reason her co-workers idolized her. Everyone from Clark Gable to Humphrey Bogart had called her his favorite leading lady.

"Devon, dear, I love your office," she announced, looking around approvingly. Paying particular attention to the lovely watercolors on the walls, she added, "You must have inherited your taste in art from your father. I never could tell one modern artist from another."

Devon smiled. She loved her mother deeply and always enjoyed her company. The fact that Sheila made a determined effort not to interfere in Devon's life made their relationship all the more pleasant. When Devon left home, Sheila sold her large house and bought condos in Beverly Hills and Palm Springs. For Devon she was the ideal mother—always there if needed, only offering advice when asked, an interesting woman pursuing her own life.

"How are you, Mother? You look marvelous."

"Thanks, dear. This is one of the things I bought when we went to Paris last year. At first I thought it was a bit much, but Helen, the nice lady who lives in the condo across the court from me, said I should make an *entrance*. After all, I haven't been on the lot for years."

Eyeing her mother's dress, Devon said, "Helen was right. You look stunning."

The dress was azure silk. Over it Sheila wore a white mink coat. Her dark hair, cut short now, framed her face in soft curls. At her throat and her ears she wore what Devon jokingly referred to as the "crown jewels," pearls and diamonds. But her only ring was the one Devon had never seen off her hand—a plain gold band.

Sheila cocked her lovely head to one side and eyed Devon carefully. "I must say, I can't quite get used to the idea of you behind that massive-desk. You still look so young to me."

"I'm thirty-four, Mother," Devon said with only slight exasperation.

"I know, but I can so clearly remember when you sat behind your little desk as a child and made paper dolls." Walking up to Devon, she hugged her quickly and said, "I *am* proud of you, darling. I wish your father could see you now. He would be so proud too."

Before Devon could make an embarrassed response, Sheila finished, "Now, let's eat. I'm starving."

When they walked into the commissary a few minutes later, Devon, as always, was amazed at the response to her mother. Heads turned and people stared unabashedly. Sheila O'Neill might have been off the screen for twenty years, but she obviously wasn't forgotten. The maître d' nearly tripped over himself pulling out a chair for the former star. To Devon's intense amusement he entirely forgot about her as he stared at her mother.

Looking around, Sheila said to Devon, "I know I say this each time, but it's changed. Everything is different —especially the people. I know it's silly, but I keep hoping to see the old crowd—Clark and Bogie and Lana. And little Elizabeth."

"Indeed." Devon laughed. "Little Eliz . . ."

At that moment an elderly man interrupted the conversation. "Miss O'Neill," he said, addressing Sheila, "I don't expect you remember me."

"Of course, I do," Sheila exclaimed, her face brightening. Turning to Devon, she explained, "This is Harry Dalton. He took all the wrinkles out of my face for my last movie."

"Oh, no, ma'am, there weren't any wrinkles to take out. And there still aren't," Dalton insisted politely. "Oh, it's such a pleasure seeing someone from the old days."

"What are you doing with yourself nowadays, Harry?"

"Same thing. Makeup. Only for these kids on tv shows." Shaking his head, he said sadly, "It's not the same. They don't make 'em like you anymore." To Devon he said reverently, "She's a star."

After a few minutes of happy reminiscing, Harry left. But just as Devon and Sheila were preparing to order, someone else came up. Throughout the meal people stopped by to talk for a moment. And everyone around them—people who were used to seeing famous actors and actresses every day on the studio lot—stared as if they'd never seen anyone like her.

When Sheila signed an autograph for one person, suddenly several besieged her.

It was quite a while before they could settle down to their lunch.

"Now, tell me about your job," Sheila urged, between bites of a delicious avocado salad.

"Well, it's a tremendous opportunity, of course. There are so many changes I want to make. I can't even begin to tell you . . ."

Sheila laughed affectionately. "Slow down, darling. Don't try to change Hollywood overnight. The movie business has been operating pretty much the same way, by its own peculiar lights, for the last seventy years. It will take a while to make a dent in those ingrained patterns."

"Well, this town's going to know I've arrived, anyway," Devon insisted.

Sheila leaned back in her chair and looked at her headstrong daughter with real concern. "They're tough, Devon, these people you'll be dealing with."

Sheila's voice, normally soft and lilting, had grown tight. Devon knew that she spoke from hard experience, and her heart went out to her.

"I know. But I can be tough, too, when I have to be. I'm my father's daughter, remember?"

"Yes." Sheila's tone had lightened. With a rueful laugh she added, "You *are* that."

In the silence that followed, Devon knew that her mother, too, was remembering the man who'd loved them both so fully.

The truth was that although Devon had never analyzed her motivation in depth, she was driven at least in part by her father's memory, by the example he had set for her. It was crucial, she felt, for Justin O'Neill's daughter to achieve something special. Anything less wouldn't do him justice. He had been one of the best agents in the business, a man admired for his intelligence and integrity in a town where both were in short supply. He had guided her mother's career so astutely that she had reached the top of her profession. If he'd lived, Devon was sure he would have made it possible for her to make the transition from sex symbol to character actress.

In a soft whisper that told Devon how much the memory touched her, Sheila said, "Once, when you were three or four and all dressed up for a birthday party, your father lifted you up and held you in his arms. Looking at me, he said, 'She's an exact replica of her beautiful mother.' I can still see that entire scene so vividly."

Then Sheila laughed softly to break the emotion of the highly charged moment. "You *were* beautiful. And, of course, I took a great deal of pride in that. But you were more than that even then. You were a leader. At that same party you organized all the other children in a game that you made up. I remember telling your father that night that you'd inherited the best of both of us."

Listening to her mother, Devon remembered something she'd read recently: "The greatest gift a man can give his children is to love their mother." Her father had certainly done that.

After a pause she said, "Wouldn't Daddy have loved this? I wish he were here right now."

"You still miss him very much, don't you?"

"Yes. He told me I could do anything, be anything. Some men wouldn't have been that encouraging."

Suddenly she remembered Spencer Tait. She knew he believed there were definite limitations on what she could achieve, what any woman could achieve.

Later, as they left the commissary, Sheila said, "It's amazing how people still remember me. I just assumed they'd all forgotten."

"Ah, but you're a star," Devon said, mimicking Harry Dalton. "They don't make them like you anymore."

"It is different now," Sheila said, sighing. "In my day it was so much more glamorous and exciting. I couldn't go to the grocery store without dressing up. A fan might see me and be disappointed that I looked ordinary."

"Mother, what if you hadn't quit?" Devon suddenly turned serious. "Many stars have stayed stars."

"Not many, darling. I felt it was better to make an exit while at least some people still wanted me to stay."

It was an ongoing discussion between the two of them. Devon understood why her mother had retired. Sheila had felt that at thirty-six she was a bit past her prime for sex-symbol roles, and it was too difficult to break the public's image of her. She'd done Ibsen, Shakespeare and other serious theatre until she'd been discovered. But once her first movie was made and she became successful, she was typecast. After that, all anyone ever saw was her figure and her spectacular beauty. She was never able to overcome that. And the powers-in-charge saw no reason to try. "If Daddy had lived, he would have changed the direction of your

career. He would have kept you a . . . star." Devon
paused and looked directly at her mother.

"No, darling, if Justin had lived, he would have
helped me become known as an *actress*. I could have
been a very good actress. But he didn't live, and I don't
regret the way we spent the life we did have." Sheila
sighed. "So many of my contemporaries, the actresses I
knew, had miserable personal lives. They went through
husband after husband, always searching for that elusive something. They were distant from their children,
who were raised by servants. And in spite of the fact
that they were constantly surrounded by a retinue, they
were desperately lonely."

"But you weren't."

"No. I was lucky." Sheila smiled.

They walked on in silence, both women remembering the same memories, reviewing the same facts.
Devon had heard the story first when just a little girl
playing "bride." Her mother had fashioned a veil for
Devon, and a playmate and had played the wedding
march from *Lohengrin* on the Steinway as the two little
girls pretended to walk down the aisle, taking turns
being the bride. Afterward, when they were alone,
Sheila had taken Devon onto her lap and, for the first
of many times, told how she and Daddy had their
wedding in the garden at Grandpapa's ranch. Everyone
had been there—Grandmother and Devon's aunts and
uncles. The wedding was in the late afternoon, in
springtime, and while it was unusual for the oranges to
blossom so early, the entire grove had been in bloom, a
mass of waxy fragrant blossoms that perfumed the air.
And, she told Devon, "When your father kissed me, he
whispered that our marriage had been made in heav-
en."

Now, remembering that well-known story, Devon
thought of the symbolism of orange blossoms. Usually

just a spray was tucked in with the bouquet or used in the headband holding the veil in place. Her mother had had an entire grove—an abundance. Devon broke the silence. "You were lucky, Mother," she said, and reached over to hug her mother. "But I think you deserved it, and I wish it could have lasted forever. For you. For me."

When she spoke, there was a catch in Sheila's voice, and Devon knew that her mother, too, had been remembering. "When you were born that Christmas Day, I thought my life was perfect. I had the best of both worlds—a career I loved and a family I adored. I knew I could be a better actress than the roles demanded, but I wasn't willing to devote that much energy to my career. I didn't want my life to be so busy that I didn't have time to devote to the people who came first in my life. Justin used to say our love was the stuff Hollywood movies were made of. And he protected that love. Then . . ." She drew a deep breath and slowly released it. She finished, ". . . he died."

She hesitated and her blue eyes misted. "I felt that he had invested so much love in you and me that it was my responsibility to maintain our family."

Devon was silent for a long moment. She understood what her mother was saying. Sheila had devoted herself to her child instead of to her career. The result was that Devon grew up secure, confident of her ability to achieve what she wished. But she had never known the kind of love her mother had known. That dream, for her, remained elusive.

Suddenly Devon felt compelled to ask a question she had never asked before. "Why didn't you remarry?"

"I did. Don't you remember? It lasted six weeks."

"I didn't mean *that*. That was a disaster, not a marriage."

"Exactly."

"But that was fifteen years ago. I know you've had offers since then, from perfectly nice men. At least two of them tried to get me to put in a good word for them."

Sheila smiled. "How silly of them. They should know mothers resent advice from daughters at least as much as daughters resent advice from mothers."

Devon laughed, then repeated, "But why didn't you marry again?"

"When my second marriage ended so quickly and unhappily, I realized something. I loved your father very much. Perhaps too much. I compared every other man I met to him, and when they couldn't measure up, that was it. So I accepted the fact that I happen to be a one-man woman." She finished, "I'm quite happy with my life, you know. I've kept my friendships with some of the old crowd, and I still study acting. And I enjoy performing with the amateur groups."

"But don't you sometimes wish you could act professionally again?" Devon pressed.

Sheila shook her head exasperatedly. "Devon, you're like a bulldog puppy, you *never* give up. I suppose that's why you're such a success now." She said pointedly, "I should be asking why you haven't married again."

Devon frowned. "That should be obvious. I didn't make a terrific success of marriage the first time I tried it."

"That wasn't *your* fault—aside from the fact you picked the wrong man. Tony was charming and I understood why you were so madly in love with him, but I'm afraid it was obvious from the beginning it would never work. He was all surface charm, Devon. There was nothing underneath. It's like what some people say about Hollywood: there's nothing behind the tinsel but tinsel. Your problem is that you're not realistic."

"Not realistic! That's ridiculous. I'm the most pragmatic person I know."

"Of course, dear, when it comes to business. But when it comes to affairs of the heart—well, I'm afraid you watched too many romantic movies as a child. Deep inside, you still expect your fantasies to come true. And I don't blame you. I'm an incurable romantic myself."

"Mother, that's silly. Long ago I learned the difference between fantasy and reality."

"Did you? Well, whatever you say, dear."

But Devon could tell by her mother's tone and the twinkle in her eyes that she didn't accept Devon's stern assertion.

When they reached Devon's office, she was surprised to find Spence waiting for her in the anteroom. He rose when he saw them and stared unabashedly at Sheila.

Feeling rather self-conscious somehow, Devon said formally, "Mother, this is Spencer Tait. Spence, this is my mother, Sheila O'Neill."

Sheila flashed one of her most winning smiles and extended a hand to Spence. As he took it he said, "I recognized you immediately, Mrs. O'Neill. I'm sure you hear it constantly, but I'm a big fan of yours."

Sheila laughed gently. "I don't hear it nearly as much as you might think. And I appreciate the compliment. I must say, I'm a tremendous fan of yours, Mr. Tait. Your films are marvelous!"

Spence looked inordinately pleased. Devon smiled wonderingly at her mother's enduring ability to charm absolutely everyone.

Glancing from mother to daughter, Spence said, "I can see where Devon gets her looks."

As Devon blushed prettily her mother shot her a shrewd glance, then looked back at Spence.

Spence continued, "Well, I don't want to interrupt. I can talk to you later, Devon."

"Please, don't go," Sheila implored. "I was just leaving. I've kept Devon far too long as it is." Kissing Devon quickly on the cheek, she said, "I'll call you later, darling." To Spence she said warmly, "It was a pleasure meeting you, Mr. Tait."

"The pleasure was all mine, ma'am," Spence insisted gallantly.

Cocking her lovely head to one side and eyeing Spence quizzically, Sheila asked, "You're not, by any chance, from Texas, are you?"

"Yes."

"I thought so. My father was a Texan, and my mother always said Texas men can charm your bloomers off." Shooting a meaningful look at Devon, Sheila finished, "Well, good-bye, all."

As she left in a cloud of white mink and subtle perfume she even had time to flash a dazzling smile at Marci.

As Spence and Devon walked into her office together he said enthusiastically, "Your mother's really something."

Devon smiled. "Most people seem to think so. You should have seen the commotion when she walked into the commissary. You'd think those people had never seen an actress before."

"They probably haven't seen one like her," Spence replied.

"Not to change the subject, but did you get the deal memo on *Last Chance*?"

"Yes. I'd like to have a meeting with you, Sally and Karl as soon as possible. Why don't you come out to my place at the beach this weekend? Bring your bathing suit in case it's warm enough to swim. We'll have dinner."

Devon hesitated. The memory of that last dinner, which had turned out to be so disturbingly unbusiness-like, remained strong. But she was well aware that business was often conducted during social occasions. To refuse Spence's invitation would look silly.

"Okay," she finally answered. "I'll call Sally and set things up for Saturday afternoon."

"Great. Come about two."

When he left, Devon tried to get down to business. But somehow she found it very difficult to concentrate.

Chapter 8

A SANTA ANA WIND, HOT AND FIERCE, BLEW THROUGH the Los Angeles Basin Thursday and Friday. By Saturday the weather was clear and warm, the temperature in the low eighties.

As Devon arrived at Spence's house in Malibu, she could see the entire curve of Santa Monica Bay. Cobalt-blue waves broke in churning white foam against pristine beaches, and there wasn't a cloud in the powder-blue sky. The Santa Ana had blown away the smog, and now everything was clean and fresh-looking.

Devon felt a sense of exhilaration. It was a perfect day for swimming, drinking chilled wine and lazing in a Jacuzzi. And for making plans for a blockbuster film.

Spence's redwood and glass beach house was separated from Pacific Coast Highway by an adobe-walled garden, and from the ocean by fifty yards of sand. When a uniformed maid admitted her, Devon looked around in surprise. It wasn't what she'd expected. It was simple, almost austere. Sunlight flooded in through floor-to-ceiling windows on the beach side. The glare from the sun and the sea was diffused inside the house, framing everything in a soft golden glow.

The house was relatively small. A large living room was filled with comfortable-looking cream-colored furniture and contemporary paintings by Hockney and Neiman. Off to one side Devon caught a glimpse of a door opening on to a bedroom. Upstairs, running the length of the house, was an open loft with a desk, file cabinets and bookcases filled to overflowing. Through an open sliding glass door Devon saw a redwood deck and lounge chairs.

The maid had immediately returned to the kitchen, where she was obviously preparing food. Delicious smells emanated from the open door.

Spence came in from the deck to greet Devon. He had just been swimming. His blond hair gleamed wetly, and drops of water glistened on his lean, tanned body. He wore only the barest of swim trunks, which rode low over his narrow hips. A thick white towel was flung carelessly over his shoulder.

For a moment Devon was taken aback. She felt a frisson of excitement as a thrill raced up her spine. Inhaling nervously, she couldn't quite meet Spence's look. But even as she looked away, pretending to study the paintings on the walls, her mind was filled with his image—taut muscles, sinewy thighs, board-flat abdomen. She felt a heightened sexual awareness more potent than anything she'd ever known.

Before either of them could speak, the doorbell rang.

As the maid came out of the kitchen, Spence said to her, "I'll get it, Betty."

It was Sally with Karl Kreiss. Sally introduced Spence quickly to the director, then they all came into the living room. Karl was a tall, thin young man, with the high-strung, nervous energy of a Thoroughbred. Though he was taller than Spence, somehow he seemed dwarfed by Spence's quiet yet compelling personality. Still, he was attractive in a way. As Devon noticed the warm looks Sally gave him, for the first time she wondered if the two were more than friends.

"I think I'll change into my suit right away," Sally said. "I don't want to miss one second of this gorgeous sunshine. How about you, Dev?"

"Not right now."

"There's a guest bedroom down that hall," Spence said. "You can change in my room if you like, Karl," he added.

"Thanks." Sally and Karl left and once more Spence and Devon were alone.

"Let's go outside on the deck," he suggested.

Nodding assent, Devon followed him outside. As she sat down on a chaise longue, Spence asked, "Would you like some wine?"

"Yes, please."

Devon was collected once more. That moment of intense attraction she'd felt in the living room was in control now. As Spence handed her a glass of chilled Sauterne, she said, "I like your house. But one thing about it confuses me."

Raising one eyebrow, he asked, "What's that?"

"There's absolutely nothing to indicate you're in the picture business. No sign of your Oscar. No pictures with actors. No bound copies of scripts." She paused to sip the cold wine. Then she finished, "It's almost as if you've made a determined effort to keep that part of your life outside."

Spence smiled. His firm mouth softened appealingly and his intense green eyes crinkled at the corners. "You're partly right," he admitted. "I enjoy my work immensely. Half the time I feel like a kid who's been turned loose in an amusement park. It's fun for me, not work. But I don't want it dominating my life. I don't want to be defined solely as a producer. Sometimes when I'm at people's houses and I see how they've surrounded themselves with the paraphernalia of the business—their own screening rooms, movie posters on the walls, framed reviews of their films—it makes me feel claustrophobic. This place is a sanctuary for me. I don't mind using it for business occasionally, like today, but not all the time. There's more to life than that."

Thinking of her own sanctuary—her house, especially her bedroom suite—Devon empathized. Not for the first time, she thought that she and Spence were surprisingly alike despite their different backgrounds.

Before she could ask him what other things filled his life, Sally and Karl came outside.

Spence rose and poured wine for both of them, then they all sat down.

"I spoke with Harrison," Devon announced. "He read the script and has okayed the project." Glancing sideways at Spence, she added, "He was especially happy to hear that it's a coventure with Spence."

"So we'll plan to shoot this winter?" Karl asked eagerly.

"If you can handle that?"

"Sure!"

Spence shot Devon a look that clearly said, "This guy's awfully certain of himself."

Ignoring it, Devon continued, "Then let's get down to planning the preproduction. You'll be working primarily with Spence, of course. After today I won't have much to do with the day-to-day operation. But if problems come up, feel free to call me anytime. I'll always be available for you. This project means a lot to me."

"We understand." Sally spoke for both herself and Karl. "Don't worry, Dev. It's going to be great!"

"I've asked Terry Bernstein to be the production

manager," Devon continued. "I think he's the best person at UFS and one of the best in town. If anyone can keep the cost down on this, he can."

Karl leaned forward and said, "You're not going to penny-pinch, are you? This should be done right, or not at all. If I'm going to make the kind of film this should be, I've got to have latitude. . . ."

"You'll have latitude," Spence interjected firmly. "I talked to Terry last night and he's drawn up a tentative budget of approximately fifteen million, not including the cost of the two leads. If we get top stars, that will mean another five to seven million." He finished dryly, "I should think twenty million dollars—and change— would give you enough latitude to produce a fairly decent film."

Karl responded to the barely veiled criticism with an angry look. Before the discussion could turn into a full-fledged argument, Devon said, "We have a tentative shooting schedule of January one through March thirtieth. That gives us sixty days in preproduction, ninety days to shoot and ninety days in postproduction. I'd like this to be our big film for the summer, to open in early July."

"Yeah," Karl agreed tersely. "Let's talk about below-the-line."

"Do you have any ideas about your art director?" Devon asked. "I know you used the same cameramen on your two previous films."

"I brought a list of people that Karl and I drew up," Sally said, taking a piece of paper from the pocket of her beach coat and placing it on the glass-topped wrought-iron table that they were all sitting around. Her tone was forcibly bright and cheerful.

It occurred to Devon that Sally was acting as referee between Karl and the people he would be working for—her and Spence. She knew that wasn't unusual, especially with temperamental young directors who chafed at restrictions placed on them by studios. There was a natural conflict between directors—whose own money wasn't involved and who wanted artistic license —and studios, who wanted to be as economical as possible with their money. But it bothered her that Karl was already showing signs of overweening egotism. And as she glanced at Spence she sensed that he was thinking the same thing.

For the next hour they went over Sally's list of possible production staff. They began with possibly the most crucial person, the art director. This artist-craftsman would determine the "look" of the movie by designing the sets and, with the help of a location manager, determining where it would be shot.

Then they discussed the position of cameraman, the cinematographer, whose key responsibility was lighting. He would bring the camera operator and focus man with him as a team. They went on to the wardrobe and makeup people, the editor and composer. Finally, by late afternoon, they had a list of people they had all agreed on.

"Now, about casting," Devon said. "As far as the four leads are concerned, the studio will want established people. With the other roles you can be more flexible in terms of casting."

"I had a young guy in mind for the role of the boy," Karl insisted. "He's from New York, so you probably won't have heard of him. But I'm telling you he's terrific."

"Okay," Devon said, determined to be fair. "We'll fly him out here and give him a test. Then we'll make a decision."

She went down the list of actors and actresses she and Spence had discussed at dinner two weeks earlier.

Looking at Karl, Spence added, "There's one thing you have to understand. The insurance company won't insure anyone who's known to use drugs heavily. All of the people on our list are clean. If you want to suggest anyone else, make sure they're clean too."

Karl's mouth tightened, his expression hardened and for a moment he looked as if he would say something derogatory.

Sally watched him nervously, then turned to Spence and said, "Don't worry. We understand."

"Good," Spence replied curtly.

To Devon's relief they all pretty much agreed on the people they wanted for the leads. Sally made a list of them in order of preference and said that first thing Monday morning she would begin calling their agents and circulating the script.

The sun was beginning to feel warm through the thin cotton of Devon's lavender T-shirt and white slacks. Excusing herself, she went into the house to change. When she emerged a few minutes later, she was wearing a lacy beach robe and under it a white maillot. The stark white of the suit accented her olive complexion. Nearly backless, it was cut high over her hips. The front dipped to a deep V, exposing a generous amount of cleavage, and was held together by thin laces.

Her mother had bought it for her when they'd vacationed together in the South of France that summer. On the French beaches, where going topless wasn't uncommon, the suit had seemed almost modest. Now Devon was uncomfortably aware of its brevity.

Spence was standing near the redwood railing that surrounded the deck, a half-empty glass of wine in his hand. When he saw Devon, his eyes were immediately drawn to the thin laces, which were more an enticement than a cover.

Devon trembled as he looked directly at her. What he was thinking was fully apparent in his appreciative gaze, and it stirred her profoundly. She felt a sudden taughtening of her breasts and instinctively pulled the robe more tightly around her. Spence said nothing, but his searing look spoke volumes.

"I think I'll try the waves a few times before dinner," Karl said. Turning to Sally, he added, "Want to join me?"

"Sure," she responded happily. She slipped off her terry cover-up, then took Karl's hand and raced down the sand with him to the water, laughing gaily.

When they were gone, Spence turned to Devon. "Let's go for a walk," he said.

Chapter 9

SETTING DOWN HER WINE GLASS, DEVON STEPPED OUT OF her sandals and followed him down the redwood steps. They didn't touch, but the space separating them was charged with electricity. They walked barefoot on the warm, soft sand to the edge of the tide line where the sand was wet and firm. The waves were breaking farther out, the foaming surf rolling in furiously. A cool breeze wafted in off the ocean, lifting Devon's hair from the nape of her neck and caressing her bare skin.

Neither Devon nor Spence spoke as they walked. They didn't feel the need to.

Though the beach had been crowded earlier, by this time it was nearly deserted. The temperature was beginning to drop. Overhead, screeching seagulls circled and dipped. Sandpipers minced along the shore on their skinny legs.

"Tell me about yourself," Spence said, turning to look at her. "What makes you tick? Ruthless ambition?'' He offered her a slow, lazy smile to take the sting out of the words.

She hesitated. But he had shared something of himself two weeks earlier when they had dinner. She could do no less now. ''You've met my mother. My father, too, was very special. He convinced me I could do anything.''

For a moment they walked in silence. Then she began talking again, slowly, explaining how her father, driving on Coldwater Canyon, had stopped to help a stalled motorist. Another car came too fast around the curve and crashed into them. ''I was twelve,'' she said, her voice soft and low.

''We share a bit of history, don't we? Losing a parent.''

Devon thought about that. They did have that in common. Although she'd had some dedicated teachers, she had not had a Ruth Ann Mayberry as he had had. But she'd had her mother, who had devoted herself to loving her child. In her early teens Devon had perceived that her parents had shared an exceptionally happy marriage. ''In spite of being widowed at a very early age, my mother . . .'' Devon stopped and smiled, shaking her head.

He was watching her and asked, ''What's to smile about?''

''I'm smiling at the idea of thirty-four being a very young age. That's my age, yet I consider myself seasoned enough to be a studio president.''

He smiled with her then, his eyes brightening with pleasure.

Devon was glad for the levity. There had been such intensity between them at each of their previous meetings. These shared moments gave them valuable insights into each other.

They walked far down the beach. By now the late-afternoon sun, a red-orange ball, was low on the horizon. They were the only people left in that area of the beach.

"Let's sit awhile. I like to sit out here and watch the sun set. The sea changes, the sky darkens—the sounds of the ocean change."

The day had been hot, and now the sky was streaked with flame slashing through the darkening lavender. The temperatures of the air and the breezes were quite cool, but Devon didn't mind. She drew the lacy beach coat closed and watched, with him, the everchanging sea and sky.

"You remember I told you about Miss Mayberry." He looked at Devon but did not wait for her to answer. "She used to say a good poet labors harder than any other kind of writer to say exactly what he means, to expose his thoughts rather than hide them. His passion for exactness is like the mathematician's. But unlike the mathematician, who thinks in abstractions, the poet not only thinks concretely but presents his thoughts concretely. See the sandpiper's tracks there in the wet sand?"

"Yes."

"And that wave . . . that one coming?"

"Yes." As Devon watched the wave crested and broke, driving the sea up along the beach in a curve of hissing, frothing foam. Then the wave, in a surge of power, gathered itself and pulled back and, once more, joined forces with the sea.

"Now that wave is once more a part of the ocean and not the beach; and the pattern of tracks is obliterated. Gone as if they had never been."

"But," Devon said, "the image of those tracks, and the sandpipers that made them, are stored in my mind."

"Especially the way the sandpipers wade out to play

'chicken' with the wave," Spence added. His enjoyment in this recollection was obvious.

Devon continued, "And the wave—building, cresting, crashing and frothing like lace trim along the hem of the beach . . ."

Suddenly, as if on signal, they faced each other, aware of their connection. They looked deep into each other's eyes and Devon ached for this man to take her in his arms. Though she watched his eyes, dark green now with emotion, she vividly pictured his mouth, his well-defined lips, and willed them to touch hers. Her heart beating furiously, she listened to the cadence of the surf's crescendo and the shrill cry of a seabird.

Spence leaned closer and Devon waited, scarcely breathing. Then, suddenly, she caught herself, and drew away, not so much physically as emotionally.

Be careful, she told herself. Remember who you are, who he is.

"You're a very special lady," Spence said, his voice a husky whisper. "Smart enough for Harrison to trust with his studio. And sensitive too."

Everything about this man pulled her to him. During each of their encounters, she'd felt a power in him as great as that in the sea surging in the background. The ocean, Devon knew, could be very beautiful when reflecting a sunny blue sky. It could be serene and calm. But it could also be dangerous and terrifying. She knew now why this man's pictures were so special. She also knew she needed to guard her emotions around him.

Quickly she stood. Trying to lighten the mood, she teased, "Weren't we invited to dinner? I'm starved."

The sun had disappeared below the horizon now, and only a rosy glow remained to soften the darkening October sky. When they had almost reached Spence's house, Devon turned to look back. There, low in the lavender twilight sky, was the evening star and, just above it, the barest beginning of a new moon. "There," she said, pointing, "is poetic imagery. That is my idea of a beautiful promise."

Spence looked at the moon, then at her, and Devon wished it could go on forever. That tranquil mood. No talk of work. No arguments. No intrusion by other people.

Fantasy time. Lavender twilight and a new moon.

But she knew reality was out there, just over the horizon. Every fantasy had to end sometime. As if on cue, reality reared its ugly head. Sally and Karl stood silhouetted in a close embrace on the deck.

"You realize they're sleeping together," Spence commented.

Devon didn't have to ask who he was referring to. "I didn't realize it until today. Still, what does it matter? It *is* their business."

"Only as long as it doesn't interfere with the film," Spence answered firmly.

Devon wanted to argue, but she knew he was right. She clenched her fists and thought, So much for fantasy.

Finally she said, "You don't like Karl, do you?"

"Do you?"

"No," she admitted reluctantly. "But I like his work. And that's all that matters."

"I agree. I'm just concerned that the person who's going to be supervising him is obviously in love with him. That doesn't help her objectivity any."

Devon stopped. She planted her bare feet on the soft sand and put her hands on her hips. Angrily she insisted, "The whole problem is that Sally's a woman, isn't it? You wouldn't question her motives or her competence if she were a man."

"Like hell I wouldn't! I'm spending ten million of my own hard-earned dollars on this film. I have a right to question her ability to handle things."

"Then don't do it! You can still back out. I'll find someone else, perhaps another studio, to do this coventure."

It wasn't an empty threat. She meant exactly what she was saying, and she saw that Spence took her seriously. For a moment anger hung like an invisible barrier between them. Devon felt brittle, as if she might snap. Spence looked tense, like a string pulled too tight. But as their eyes met and held each other immobile once more, there was a subtle change. The anger dissipated. And in its place was capitulation, though Devon wasn't entirely sure which of them was surrendering and which was claiming victory.

"Okay," Spence said simply. "But I won't give her free reign. I'll watch this production like a hawk."

"I wouldn't expect anything else," Devon replied.

Slowly a smile spread across his face, softening the features that had been cold and hard only a moment before. "Do you ever give in?" he asked. There was a sly glint in his green eyes, and Devon knew the question held a potent double meaning.

She held her breath. Suddenly all of her determination seemed to evaporate under the heady impact of that ironic smile and those emerald eyes.

"Sometimes," Devon finally answered. It was a whisper, and a promise.

As Devon was unlocking her front door that night, she heard her phone ringing. Hurriedly opening the door, she dropped her beach tote on the floor and ran to the phone.

"Hello," she said breathlessly.

Somehow she had been convinced it was Spence. When her mother's voice responded happily, "Hello, darling," she felt a stab of disappointment.

"You sound out of breath," Sheila continued.

"I was just unlocking the door when you rang,"

Devon explained. "I was out at Spencer Tait's beach house."

"Oh?" Sheila managed to convey a great deal of meaning in that one brief word.

"We were having a meeting about *Last Chance,*" Devon explained. "Sally Challis and Karl Kreiss, the director, were there too."

"I see."

Devon thought she detected a note of disappointment in her mother's voice. But Sheila continued breezily, "I just wanted to let you know I'm going to the Bahamas for a couple of weeks. But I'll be back for Thanksgiving. Your grandparents are coming down this year."

"That will be nice," Devon said sincerely. She liked her grandparents and wished she saw them more often.

"Why don't you invite Spencer Tait to join us?"

"Mother, I hardly know him that well."

"I understand he has no family, and I just thought . . ."

"I know very well what you thought," Devon replied.

"Did you have a pleasant day?" Sheila asked innocently, ignoring the barbed reply.

"Yes," Devon admitted. "It was beautiful in Malibu. Aside from a few minor problems the meeting went well. The movie's looking good, I think."

"Since you're getting back rather late, I assume you stayed for dinner."

"Yes, Mother." Devon said nothing further, but she thought about that dinner. The maid had prepared it, then left. It didn't surprise Devon that Spence preferred not to have live-in servants. Afterward Devon had made a point of leaving when Sally and Karl did because she knew it would be dangerous to stay.

Speaking more to herself than to her mother, Devon

said thoughtfully, "Spence isn't like most people in the business. He operates from strength, not from insecurity."

"Beware, love, that's a rare quality to find. And once found, it's hard to turn your back on it."

Sheila's tone was teasing, but Devon knew she was actually quite serious.

Sheila continued, "That's why I fell in love with your father. And it's why I'm so reluctant to try to replace him in my life. It's a bit like trading fourteen-carat gold for gold plate."

"In Hollywood you're much more apt to find imitations, rather than the real thing," Devon replied dryly.

"Ah, but those imitations can be seductive. Glamor, no matter how superficial, can be awfully enticing."

Devon thought of Tony. She had certainly been seduced by him, his sheer physical perfection, his aura of strength and substance. But it was entirely superficial. Fool's gold. And she'd been the fool. Comparing him now to Spence, she wondered how she could ever have thought herself so deeply in love with Tony.

Spence had the most potent combination of attributes a man can have—strength and sensitivity. He was artistic, in tune with emotion, beauty; yet at the same time he had the tensile strength of steel. He had been annealed by the hardships of his life, toughened without being hardened.

As Devon remained silent, Sheila finished, "Well, dear, I'll let you go. What would you like me to bring you back from the islands?"

Devon smiled. "Just yourself. Take care."

"I will, darling. 'Bye."

After hanging up, Devon picked up the tote she'd dropped on the floor, then took it into her bedroom. As she unpacked it, a few grains of sand fell out. Running the tiny, hard crystals over her fingers, she remembered that walk on the beach. She yearned for Spence then, longed for the kiss that she might have had.

And she realized that although she'd run away from an explosive situation that night, she might not be able to do so again.

Chapter 10

THE OLD GIRLS' NETWORK CONVENED FOR ITS MONTHLY meeting the second Monday in November. There were roughly two hundred women in the banquet room of the venerable old Beverly Wilshire Hotel on Wilshire Boulevard in the heart of Beverly Hills. Devon spoke briefly, then answered questions from the group. Most of the questions were variations on a single theme—how she had gotten where she was.

She tried to be completely honest, to avoid simplistic answers. Hard work and talent weren't enough, she admitted. But beyond that she could only say, "The old male-dominated power structure is vulnerable now. The walls are crumbling. Keep trying, and you'll have a better chance of making it than you've ever had before."

When she had finished, she joined Sally at the bar for a drink.

"Look who I found," Sally said with a grin.

Next to her was Rebecca Dennison, who, with

Devon, had helped found the group. She was an attorney.

"So the three-martini lunches start," Rebecca said with a sly smile as Devon downed a Bloody Mary.

"I've earned this," Devon replied. "I'm beginning to think that if I have to answer one more question about women making it in Hollywood, I'm going to chuck the whole thing and run off to Tahiti. *Time* and *Newsweek* have both been after me for interviews. To say nothing of the trades, the LA *Times*, the *Herald-Examiner*, and *The Wall Street Journal*."

"*The Wall Street Journal?* Mmm, you've definitely arrived," Rebecca replied.

"You're a media personality now," Sally added. "You've got to accept the press as a necessary evil."

"Never. I wish they'd just let me do my job in peace."

"Let's get out of here," Rebecca said, as they were jostled by other women pressing against the bar.

"Good idea," Devon agreed.

A few minutes later they were sitting at a small table in the El Pedrino Room, an intimate little bar just off the hotel lobby.

When the waiter took their order, Devon asked for Perrier. In response to Rebecca's knowing smile, she said, "Well, I can't very well start going back to work drunk after only a month on the job."

As their laughter subsided Sally flashed Devon a meaningful look. Devon knew what it meant. She and Sally had been hoping to run across their friend at the meeting, and now was the time to broach the plan they had formulated.

"Becky, how would you like to come to work at UFS?" Devon asked without preamble.

Rebecca's look of surprise lasted for only the briefest moment. Then she smiled broadly. "I'd love to!"

"All right!" Sally exclaimed. "The Three Musketeers at UFS."

Devon laughed, too, filled with an exhilarating sense of camaraderie. Rebecca wasn't a close personal friend, like Sally, but she was someone Devon admired a great deal. Her pale blond loveliness masked a tendency to go for the jugular that astonished her male colleagues. She wasn't easily beaten in a legal fight, and Devon knew she would be a valuable asset in the business affairs department.

"I'll give my notice today and be at work in two weeks," Rebecca said.

"Good. I'll notify Charlie Woods, the vice-president in charge of business affairs."

"So what have you been up to, Becky?" Sally asked, sipping her drink.

"I just got back from a weekend in Tahoe with a junior partner at my firm. I'm *still* exhausted. I don't think I got more than six hours sleep all weekend."

"Is this guy serious or just the usual?"

"The usual, of course," Rebecca answered Sally with typical outspokenness. "Now that I'm going to UFS, he's part of my past, not my future."

"I'm glad your future is with UFS," Devon said with real sincerity.

"So am I. Starting something new is always exciting. I guess that's why I prefer new loves to old ones." Rebecca's tone was whimsical.

Devon laughed, but Sally looked just a bit disapproving. When it came to sexual relationships, she and Rebecca had always disagreed strongly. Rebecca was a free spirit who had no inclination for marriage. She thought it boring and restrictive. Sally, however, was an incurable romantic whose longing for commitment and security had only been increased by her divorce.

Suddenly Sally asked, "Are you going to that fete

honoring Jimmy Stewart at the Ahmanson Theatre, Dev?"

"Yes. Would you like a ticket?"

"Yes. Two if that's okay."

"Sure."

Rebecca shot Devon a shrewdly appraising look. "Who are you going with, Dev?"

"God only knows. I haven't even thought about it."

"You're in a touchy situation, you know."

"What do you mean?"

"You can't go out with someone in an inferior position. And most of the men on your level are married. It's all right for married men to fool around in this business. Sometimes I think it's required of them to prove they're not gay. But it's not all right for women in your position."

Devon was uncomfortably reminded of what Spence had told her that night at the Beverly Hills Hotel. "The same rules and regulations don't apply to women."

For the first time Devon came to terms fully with what her job meant to her personal life. If she was to go out socially with Spence, if she had an affair with him, it would be widely discussed. She knew exactly how the gossip would run: There would be talk that she was sleeping with him merely to keep him at UFS. There would be speculation that Spence was sleeping with her merely to get a more lucrative contract with the studio.

There would be clear conflict of interest on her part and questions of motive on Spence's. Everyone at the studio would discuss the situation with relish. And the people who wanted her job would try to use the situation to somehow undermine her position.

Yes, she thought, everyone would find it fascinating. Everyone except Harrison. I don't think that's what he had in mind when he told me to get along with Spence.

The thought of having her most intimate feelings and

actions open to such scrutiny and gossip was unbearable.

"You're looking awfully pensive," Rebecca observed.

Glancing up, Devon realized she'd been lost in thought. Both Rebecca and Sally were watching her with interest.

"I was just thinking I should turn celibate," Devon joked.

"Oh, Dev, it can't be that bad," Sally insisted. "Rebecca's exaggerating. Love and career don't have to be mutually exclusive."

"You always were a Pollyanna, Sally." Rebecca's tone was friendly but blunt. "For women, mixing sex and business is a time bomb."

"That's certainly a grim assessment," Sally replied.

"It's a realistic one. I'll tell you what happens when you become involved with someone you work with. When the relationship goes sour, as it usually does, it's the woman who's let go. It's unfair, but that's the way it is. That's one reason I have no intention of getting serious with that junior partner. And just try having an affair with someone your boss thinks might compromise you. It's tolerated when a man puts his starlet–girl friend in a movie. If Devon tried the same thing, Harrison Kahn would be down on her like a shot."

"Rebecca, that's ridiculous," Sally argued with surprising vehemence. "You're saying that when women reach positions of authority they've got to forget about falling in love, except in certain rigidly defined instances."

"Exactly. It's the old sexual double standard."

"But the men we're most likely to meet, and find interesting, are the ones we're working with."

"True. Just be careful who you get serious about."

"I don't agree with you," Sally insisted.

"Well, look at your own experience with Jerry. You both worked at Donovan. Which one of you left when the marriage ended?" Rebecca pointed out matter-of-factly.

Devon stepped in before the disagreement could erupt into a full-fledged argument.

"We've all got to be getting back to work."

Rebecca left then, and Sally and Devon drove back to the studio in Sally's BMW. Both women were silent, distracted. Devon knew very well why Rebecca's hard words had upset Sally. In her own mind she was profoundly disturbed by Rebecca's assertion. For she suspected Rebecca was right.

Back in her office Marci gave Devon a sheaf of messages. Among them was a call from Spence saying that the rough cut of his new film, *Images*, was going to be screened at two-thirty. The movie, a highly erotic love story, had been of special interest to Devon since she first read the script a week earlier. She told Marci where she could be reached, then hurried down to the screening room in the basement floor.

This particular screening room was one of the original ones built fifty years earlier, when the studio was under construction. The chairs were large, plush, red-leather armchairs. It was a miniature theatre. There were about ten rows of the plush seats descending to a screen that filled the wall at the end of the room.

The bottom three rows of seats were filled with people who Devon knew must be members of the cast and crew on *Images*. Spence sat alone in the top row next to the control panel, which allowed him to communicate with the projectionist. He stood as Devon approached.

"Good afternoon. Glad you were free for this. I hear you've been busy these past couple of weeks."

"Busy enough." Devon softened her words with a smile. "This 'mogul' business is very demanding. I hardly have time to do my nails, wash my hair and run the studio too."

She was pleased to hear his low laugh. "I'm really looking forward to seeing this," she said, sitting down.

As he settled into the seat next to her he turned the full force of his green eyes on her. He smiled that slow, lazy smile that registered mostly in his eyes, finally reaching the corners of his mouth. "I'm looking forward to your viewing it too."

He pushed a button and said into the intercom, "You can start now." Then he turned back to Devon. "I'll be interested in your professional evaluation, of course. But I'm also curious to see if it has evocative qualities for you."

The lights went off. Then a narrow beam of light from the tiny projectionist's window cut through the pitch blackness to illuminate the screen.

The rough cut of the film didn't include music or sound effects. Thus, the film began in utter silence as the credits rolled across the screen. They began with the familiar legend "A Spencer Tait film."

The remaining credits—the actors, writer, director, et cetera—flashed across.

As the last credit disappeared from the screen Spence leaned close to Devon and, dropping his voice to a whisper, said, "I've thought a lot about you these past two weeks. That was a good day at my house. And the best part was the walk on the beach."

He settled back in the seat and crossed one leg comfortably over the other.

Devon heard "I've thought a lot about you" play through her mind over and over again.

And I've thought a lot about *you*, she thought. But you didn't call and I couldn't call you.

Suddenly Devon forced herself to stop, to forget that he was so close she could catch his special scent. He was so strong a personality, despite that deceptively quiet manner, that she could feel him breathe in the darkness.

She concentrated on the screen. It was a simple plot. A young woman from New York, an ambitious, highly charged executive on vacation in Greece, meets a young Greek painter who for the first time opens up her repressed sensual nature, helping her to come to terms with her sexuality. When, in the end, the woman leaves her high-pressured, lonely existence for a simpler, more satisfying life with the painter, the audience has a sense of the rightness of her decision.

The script was based on a novel by one of the most respected writers in the English language. The film could have been merely opportunistic, trading on cheap sensationalism and the novel's racy reputation. But it went far beyond that. It had depth of characterization, poignancy and an almost lyrical beauty. Far from being just another sexy movie, it was a true work of art. As the story unfolded Devon marveled at the beautiful cinematography and the excellent performances of the two leads, both newcomers. It was a well-written script, literate and insightful, with just enough humor to keep it from being too heavy-handed.

The nudity was cleverly handled. The audience didn't actually see as much as it thought it was seeing—just a curve of hip, a long length of bare legs entwined, muscular shoulders pressing down against full breasts.

But as the sexual scenes became more explicit, Devon felt her cool objectivity waver. It did, indeed, have evocative qualities for her, especially when the hero and heroine walked along the beach, not touching, just talking, but clearly desiring each other deeply.

Gradually Devon became more and more aware of Spence sitting so close beside her. In the darkness she couldn't even make out his features. But she could feel his shoulders brushing hers. At one point he shifted his legs, and his thigh touched hers briefly. Through the thin silk of her dress, she felt the taut muscles of his thigh. Startled by the jolt of electricity that the brief contact elicited, she shot him a quick look. But he was staring ahead at the screen—as far as she could tell.

On screen the black-haired, deeply tanned hero was making love to the blond, fair-skinned heroine on a deserted beach. As Devon watched it occurred to her that she and Spence would contrast in just the same way, only she would be dark against his lighter skin.

Without being consciously aware of what was happening, Devon lost herself in the scene, imagining that it was she and Spence making love on the warm, soft sand. In the utter darkness and silence of the room, it was like a daydream come true, very vivid, very intimate.

Now, she thought, he is looking at me. There is a command in his eyes that I can't disobey. His hand is lifting my dress slowly, very slowly. Finally I am naked before him. His hands begin exploring, caressing, sliding over the curves of my body. His touch is gentle, the way one lightly strokes velvet or silk. . . .

First his fingertips trace the fullness of my breasts, lingering to circle the hardening nipples. I am flooded with delicious new sensations. I feel a voluptuous suspense that seeks not fulfillment but prolongation. . . .

Now his fingertips are running lightly past my waist to my stomach. They pause to circle slowly, provocatively. I am dissolving under his touch, melting, becoming lighter than air. I am trembling, helpless under this tender onslaught. . . .

His green eyes are watching me carefully and he knows exactly what I desire, my most secret longings. He looks at me and he *knows*. . . .

Then he kisses me again and again, until I am drunk with his kisses. It leaves me tingling, reeling, wanting more and more and more. . . . Finally his mouth cov-

ers mine in one interminable kiss and I nearly lose
consciousness. . . .

Then his mouth is on my throat, in the hollow
between my breasts, as his fingertips tighten on my
hips, drawing me closer and closer. I'm enveloped in
his lovemaking, an endless dream. . . .

The scene dissolved into another. Devon shook
herself out of her reverie. It had only lasted a few
seconds, she knew, this all-too-vivid daydream. Yet, it
had seemed like hours. She felt spent, as if they had
actually made love.

The movie dissolved on the screen a few minutes
later in a slow fade to black. In an instant the lights
were on, flooding the room with a harsh, yellow glare.
The intimacy of the darkness was destroyed.

Devon blinked once before she grew accustomed to
the light. Turning to look at Spence, she found him
watching her intently. She felt her eyes shining brightly
as she met his look, as if she had a sudden fever. A
shiver passed down her back, touching every nerve.

This is how I felt at *Gone With the Wind,* she
remembered. The same delicious shiver of anticipa-
tion. . . .

A smile hovered at his lips. But his eyes were like
green fire lit by an erotic flame. The combination of the
erotic and the tender was explosive.

Then someone spoke, and the highly charged moment was defused. It had only lasted for a second or
two but had seemed an eternity as green eyes were
locked into blue ones, filled with the awareness of
profound desire.

Reluctantly Spence turned away to answer the person who had spoken to him. Devon pulled herself
together. She reminded herself of who she was, where
she was. As she walked out of the screening room next
to Spence, she said nothing.

Finally, in the hallway, she said to him, "The movie's

stunning." She was surprised at how calm her voice sounded, for inside her emotions were churning.

"Thank you." His eyes held hers spellbound once more, and she knew there was a great deal more he wanted to say. But this wasn't the time or the place.

"Well . . . good-bye," she finally murmured. But as she walked away, she felt his eyes following her.

So now it's obvious, Devon thought forlornly as she rode the elevator alone up to the third floor. I think I've always known it, even when we first met and hated each other on sight.

Suddenly she remembered something she'd heard once long before: "The things you come to love best are the things you didn't love at first."

She loved Spencer Tait, though she still knew so little about him. She desired him with a passion so intense, it seemed to ignite her very soul. Yet, they had never touched. Not once.

What would his touch do to me, she wondered, if his mere look can shake me to my very core?

Chapter 11

DEVON STOOD ON THE TERRACE OF HER SUITE AT BLAKES Hotel. As her hands lightly held the black wrought-iron railing, she looked out over the Kensington rooftops. On this late November evening, London was swathed in a luminous gray mist. Devon loved this city—it was old, charming, peaceful somehow. It had none of the impersonal, cold modernity of cities like New York and Los Angeles.

She almost felt she'd stepped into a fairy tale as she looked out at the rows of brick town houses on this narrow street off the King's Road. Blakes was a small, intimate hotel, a favorite of the film community. It actually occupied town houses on both sides of the street.

Devon's suite was on the top floor of the building. There was a sitting room and a small kitchen, and a winding stairway that led up to the bedroom on the second story. Decorated in 1930's art deco style, it was light, comfortably modern yet charming. When she'd first seen the suite, she'd half expected to see Fred Astaire and Ginger Rogers come dancing in off the terrace in a flourish of tuxedo and swirling chiffon.

Suddenly she shivered. This winter evening was cold and she wasn't dressed for it. She was wearing a stunning black silk evening gown covered with cobwebby gold filigree lace. That night was the royal premiere of Spence's movie *Jacks*, and Devon had dressed in her very best. After the movie she and Spence, along with the stars of the film, would be presented to the Queen.

It had been a hectic trip. They'd arrived late Friday night and were immediately plunged into a series of social events and business meetings that lasted throughout the weekend. It was now Monday evening. The following morning they would return to LA.

This was an important trip for Devon because it was the first time she had publicly represented the studio and the first time she had met the studio's foreign executives. She felt confident she had done well so far. And she had thoroughly enjoyed meeting many of the people in the British movie industry.

Yet, throughout the weekend, she had been aware of a subtle undercurrent between herself and Spence. It was charged with a sexual tension that was barely in check.

It started on the flight to London. They hadn't sat together. Each had work to do and they had brought their secretaries. But throughout the long flight, one would catch the other glancing across the wide first-class compartment. There would be brief eye contact, an intense moment of awareness, then downcast eyes and averted gazes.

During the myriad meetings and parties it was the same. Devon was constantly aware of Spence's presence, even when he was out of sight across a crowded room.

Thus, Devon had been careful never to be alone with him, never to allow herself one moment of free time.

Suddenly someone knocked at the door. Devon knew it was probably the chauffeur of the limousine that was due to take her and the others to the theatre. Grabbing an ankle-length black mink cape, she opened the door.

Spence stood there, hands thrust casually in the pockets of his black tuxedo. He looked absolutely wonderful—lean, elegant, the antithesis of his normally casual appearance.

Devon's eyes opened wide in surprise, and her lips parted slightly.

Before she could speak, he said nonchalantly, "I thought we'd go to the theatre together."

"What about Ben and Maureen?" Devon asked, referring to the stars of the film.

"Oh, they're going in a separate car. They wanted to make an entrance of course." Glancing at his watch, he finished, "We'd better be going."

Devon's temper flared at his presumption in changing the arrangements she had made so carefully. "We were supposed to go together. Just what the hell do you think you're doing . . . ?"

"I'm accommodating a couple of egotistical actors," Spence snapped.

"If there's any accommodating to be done, *I* should be the one to do it. I'm in charge."

"Damn it, I know you're in charge, Devon. You're the boss! Believe me, I wasn't trying to usurp your authority by letting Ben and Maureen have their little moment in the spotlight alone."

His eyes were flashing dark emerald green and his tone was barely civil.

In a flash of insight Devon realized that he thought she was pulling rank on him, and he resented it deeply.

Well, that was exactly what she was doing, she knew. Trying to put a safe distance between them by reminding him that she was his boss.

"You're right. We'd better be going," she finally said coolly.

She walked beside him down the hallway, then entered the tiny elevator with him. In the small, enclosed space his presence was even more disturbing. Devon stared determinedly at the elevator door, but she was excruciatingly aware of Spence watching her silently. His look held a lingering anger and something more—something far more potent than anger.

As the door opened on the ground floor he said with a quiet intensity, "You look lovely."

It was the simplest of compliments. Yet, it affected Devon like a glass of Dom Pérignon. She hesitated, feeling almost lightheaded. Finally she forced herself to walk calmly out of the elevator. A moment later she and Spence were sitting in the back seat of the limousine.

Devon tried not to think about how tantalizingly close he was. She stared determinedly out the window at the passing scenery. Chelsea was her favorite area of London, a pleasant residential section of fountains and plane trees and town houses fronted by tiny gardens. But that night she couldn't concentrate on it. She hardly noticed when they arrived at the Odeon Theatre in Leicester Square.

An excited, milling throng packed the area in front of the theatre. Spence took Devon's arm and led her down the roped off area that had been cleared for the theatregoers. Helmeted bobbies kept back the crowd. Most of the people, Devon knew, had come to see the actors in the film, as well as the Queen herself.

Inside, Devon and Spence sat down in the opulent theatre, which dated from the 1930's. Immediately

Spence leaned over and unclasped her cape. His fingers lingered just a moment at her breast before arranging the cape over the back of the plush seat.

Devon felt a rush of emotions—surprise, pleasure, embarassment.

Then the bugles blew a fanfare and Devon watched as the Queen led the dignitaries into the Royal Enclosure. A moment later the movie began.

Devon had already seen *Jacks*, a heartwarming story of innocent yet profound adolescent love, and had liked it tremendously.

Relax, she told herself, enjoy this experience. You may never get another chance to sit in a theatre with a queen.

But as she sat next to Spence, she was uncomfortably reminded of the last time she had viewed a film with him and the erotic fantasies that had thrilled her then.

What does he have in mind? she wondered as the movie unfolded. We weren't supposed to come together. Or leave together.

It seemed an eternity before the movie ended. Devon and Spence made their way through the departing crowd to the private room where they were presented to the Queen. Devon found her surprisingly petite and friendly. Afterward they went to a supper party in the ballroom of the venerable Claridge's Hotel, hosted by the foreign executives of UFS.

Devon saw little of Spence during the party. Both of them were surrounded by well-wishers and people trying to curry favor. Occasionally Devon caught Spence's eye, and their gazes would lock for one timeless moment. Then someone else would intervene and the moment would be lost.

Finally, at nearly two o'clock in the morning, the crowd began to thin. The people speaking to Devon became less insistent. She was just depositing her empty glass of champagne on a waiter's tray that was piled with empty glasses when she felt Spence at her side.

"Ready to leave?" he asked.

"Yes."

She took her leave of the few remaining executives, then went out to the waiting limousine with Spence. As she leaned back in the seat, enveloped by the warmth of the mink cape, she felt tired and yet excited. The evening, she knew, was far from over.

A few minutes later, as she stood in front of the door of her suite, Spence gently took her key from her hand and unlocked the door. He had said nothing during the short ride back from Claridge's. He said nothing now. But the look in his eyes was unmistakable.

Devon entered the sitting room and heard the door click softly as Spence closed it behind him.

She turned to face him. Her entire attitude, the stiff way she held her body, the half-fearful look on her face, made her look for all the world as if she were facing the most difficult challenge of her life. In a way she was. Her job dictated that she remain businesslike with this compelling man. Her heart urged her to seize the moment. Her full lower lip trembled slightly. She opened her mouth to speak, then stopped. She had no idea what to say.

And still he continued to watch her silently, his green eyes staring into her widening blue ones. His gaze smoldered as it locked with the half-fearful, half-expectant look in hers.

Slowly, with an unhurried air, he crossed the sitting room to where she stood holding her hands in tight balls at her sides. Cupping her chin in one hand, with the other he tenderly traced her features. His fingertips lightly trailed over her cheeks, the bridge of her short, upturned nose, her fine, thin brows.

"Please, don't." She drew back.

He silenced her by placing his fingertips gently on her

lips. "Forget the studio. Forget who you are and who I am. I know what you're thinking and it doesn't matter. Nothing in the world matters tonight but you and me."

But Devon clung desperately to the last fragile thread of her self-control. She *couldn't* love this man. The price was too high.

"No!" she almost shouted. Then, in a softer voice, she said, "Please go."

But she didn't move away from him. She couldn't. She was trapped halfway between reason and passion.

His whole expression changed. His eyes were emerald fire, his face an implacable mask of determination. With a tiny shudder of fear, she realized he wasn't about to be put off by her empty protests.

Slowly he shook his head. "No, Devon. I've been half-crazy with wanting you for weeks. And whether you admit it or not, I know you want me. You're not my boss tonight. You're a woman."

With one sudden, graceful move he swept her off her feet and into his arms. Holding her securely, he began mounting the stairs to the bedroom.

"Put me down!" she demanded, but he might as well have been deaf. "If you're trying to prove your masculinity because your ego can't handle working under a woman . . ." she began, but the razor-edged sarcasm of her words was also lost on him. He seemed not to feel the pain she was trying to inflict on him to stop him from completing the seduction she both wanted and feared.

They were in the bedroom now. Without stopping to turn on the light, he crossed the room and laid her down on the bed. Moonlight streamed in through the windows. The bed was turned down, and Devon felt the satin sheets cool and smooth through the thin lace of her dress.

He sat beside her, his hands planted firmly on either side of her waist, trapping her.

"If you're going to resort to rape . . ." Devon began, her voice shaky.

"I'm not going to rape you. I would never hurt you. But I do intend to love you, thoroughly and well."

He moved toward her and she flinched. But he merely kissed her, long and sweetly. Behind the gentle touch, the light contact of his lips on hers, throbbed a powerful surge of emotion.

She felt the same exquisite electricity she'd felt in the screening room. Only this was no fantasy; it was real. She knew that she would be loved all the night through by this man, loved completely, without restraint. She would be fulfilled in spite of herself.

Devon sighed deeply. Her body relaxed as she gave up the fight, which she had never really expected to win. For she had been fighting her own fierce passion as well as Spence's.

She smiled and asked wistfully, "Will you make all my fantasies come true?"

"Every one."

He was teasing now, a wry smile playing around the corners of his lips. Yet, underneath the sudden tenderness, she knew he meant what he said. And she felt a rush of exultation. This night would be like no other.

"Tell me your most secret fantasy," he urged, his voice a whisper in the silent room.

Her fantasy was every woman's: to be loved so completely, so well, that she would know not only the man but herself as well. Her fantasy was to be touched in the most secret, most hidden part of her psyche. To know no boundaries to her passion. To be set free from inhibition.

She placed her hands on his face in the same manner he had done and kissed him, as softly and sweetly as he had kissed her. Just the lightest touch. Just a promise of what was to be. Then she reached out her hand and laced her fingers with his.

And she talked to him her voice was a husky whisper in the darkness. She told him things she had never told any man. When she saw the expression in his eyes, she knew he understood.

As she talked to him his hand moved slowly down her side. Through the gossamer-thin fabric of her evening gown she felt the pulsating touch of his fingertips.

"Do you know when I first wanted you?" she asked, breathless from the effect of his deliberate sensuality.

"Yes." He smiled slyly at her look of surprise. "I know perfectly well when you first wanted me. And let me tell you, if we'd been alone on that beach, I'd have made love to you then and there."

She arched her eyebrows. "Would you, now? And what makes you think I could be taken so easily?"

"I don't think you could be taken easily. I just know that you can be taken by me."

"Why you conceited, overbearing . . ."

Before she could finish, he laughed lustily and grabbed the fists she had raised to his chest. "Stop fighting, my little witch. *You're* the victor in this battle of wills."

Devon relaxed in his arms. Her fingers unclenched and she pressed them against his chest, loving the feel of him. "Ah, no, Spencer Tait. If anyone's won, it's you."

He pulled her against him. His lips lightly brushed her closed eyelids, her cheekbones, before finally reaching her lips. He kissed her deeply, his tongue penetrating the soft moistness of her mouth. She felt she'd been waiting all her life for that moment. Her heart pounded and her lips parted even farther as she opened herself to him completely, without reservation.

She moaned, a low animal sound deep in her throat, as her body melded to his. Her hands left his chest and moved upward to his neck. Her fingertips threaded through the thick golden hair that brushed his collar.

She was almost unbearably sensitive to every delicious sensation—the silky feel of his hair on her fingertips, his mouth firm, demanding yet tender against hers.

She pressed more tightly against him. Her body clung to his and her limbs quivered. She felt that she couldn't get close enough to him. Her breasts tautened against his chest. Suddenly clothes were an irritating barrier. She wanted to feel his skin against hers, to have nothing between them.

"Spence . . ." she whispered. Her voice sounded drugged. And it was—drugged with desire. She had never wanted a man as she wanted this one. She felt totally wanton, as if his potent virility had exorcised every last inhibition from her yearning body.

He pulled back a few inches—just enough to look deep into her eyes. What he saw there made his own eyes glint with a green fire ignited by passion.

She knew that with him she could explore every facet of her sensual being, fulfill every fantasy she'd ever had.

She rose, then stood proudly in front of him as he sat on the edge of the bed. While he watched, she slowly unzipped the gown, then let it fall in a crumpled heap of silk at her feet. As she stepped out of it she kicked off the black satin pumps.

She was wearing shimmering silk stockings attached to lace-covered garter straps. And above that, a strapless black merry widow of ribbon and lace over the tiniest silk bikini panty.

Spence's eyes widened in surprise and pleasure. "I feel like I've slipped back in time a century or more and I'm stealing a night with the king's own courtesan."

Devon smiled shyly. "I told myself I intended to

resist you. But I think when I dressed tonight, I dressed for *you*."

His eyes roved hungrily over her scantily clad body as she stood inches from him. Her full breasts nearly overflowed the brief demicups. Her gently rounded hips were visible under the lace-edged garment.

With exquisite deliberateness she unhooked one garter at a time, then slowly rolled down the silk stockings, first one, then the other. Then she straightened and, still keeping her eyes locked into Spence's, she began unbuttoning the brief corselet itself.

As Spence watched Devon performed a slow strip tease. There were tiny hooks all the way down the front. Her fingers carefully undid one hook at a time. When the first was open, the corselet parted slightly, revealing even more of her breasts. When the second was opened, it parted still farther. Now only the very tips of her breasts were hidden from Spence's eyes. As she released the third hook her breasts came free. Her nipples were already hard with barely suppressed desire.

Spence's mouth softened in the merest whisper of a smile.

Slowly Devon continued. Her waist, slender and soft, was revealed. Then her stomach. Finally the last hook was undone and she let the corselet fall to the floor.

She was naked now save for the tiny bikini panty, which was no more than a silky black ribbon across the very bottom of her hips.

"Come here," Spence commanded softly.

Devon stepped closer until she was a mere hair's breadth from him. He reached up, hooked a finger in each side of the sensuous lace panty and slowly slid it down her slender thighs, past her quivering knees, till it finally dropped onto the floor with the rest of her clothes. His hands traveled back up her legs and thighs, stopping to grip her hips possessively.

Leaning forward, he kissed the tender skin just above the triangle of dark, curly hair.

A shiver ran through Devon's body, rocking her to the very depths of her being. She placed her hands on his broad shoulders, then slowly knelt down in front of him. Now she was looking up at him and his hands were resting gently on her smooth, sloping shoulders.

They looked at each other for a long moment, then he lifted her up onto the bed, next to him. He began to loosen his tie, but Devon placed her fingers over his to stop him.

"No, love. Let *me*," she whispered.

She undressed him with the same careful deliberation she had shown with her own clothes. First she loosened the tie at his throat. Then she pulled off his jacket, allowing herself the luxury of letting her fingers trail across his broad shoulders. His shirt came next. When his broad, smooth chest was bare, she rained tiny, feather-light kisses across it.

When she reached down to unhook the band of his trousers, his stomach muscles clenched spasmodically at her touch. A moment later the trousers were off, and Devon was delightfully shocked to discover that he wore nothing underneath.

His powerful pectoral muscles looked almost as if they'd been sculpted by a master artist. Her eyes roamed lower, to his flat abdomen, then to his lean, masculine hips. His legs were long, sinewy.

Her fingers splayed over his heaving chest. His breath caught in his throat as her hands continued to explore him unashamedly. But when she reached his narrow waist, she stopped as he shuddered.

She buried her face against him then, luxuriating in the feel of him, his clean, musky male scent. A soft whimper of pleasure escaped her lips.

Lying down, he pulled her into the curve of his body. For the first time she felt her bare skin against his, from her quivering breasts straining against his hard chest to her toes flexing against his. Being so close to him, wanting desperately to be even closer, was the most exquisite agony in the world.

With a hunger that was voracious he took her mouth, his lips insistent, almost brutal, as he tasted her yielding sweetness. She parted her lips to meet his demand. Her fingers gripped his shoulders, the nails digging into his firm flesh.

As his mouth explored hers, Devon knew there was nothing she could deny him. Tonight she wasn't the president of United Film Studios but a woman finding the fulfillment she'd always dreamed of. A woman in love.

Spence's eyes turned a dark emerald green as he paused to look down at her. Her breasts rose and fell against his chest.

"Devon"—his voice was a throaty whisper in the silent room—"your body's as beautiful as your name."

"It's yours," she answered. "Every inch."

"Then I'll have to explore my new territory," he said with a wry smile. The smile faded as he continued more intently, "God! Devon, if you knew how you look right now . . . your hair like a dark halo against the white of the pillow. You *are* a witch, you know. That gown you wore tonight was appropriate—bewitching black."

She smiled, glorying in her femininity. "I hope I've cast a spell over you. One that only daylight can break."

"Nothing can break this spell."

"Then you've only yourself to blame, Spencer Tait. Because you make me feel absolutely magical."

"I mean to make you feel a great many things before this night is done," he said.

In the depths of his eyes she could see how profoundly he wanted her. Her breath caught, then her mouth was covered by his. Reluctantly his lips left hers to trail down her throat, his tongue flicking lightly at her skin.

As he'd said he would, he explored her thoroughly, his lips seeking the tender hollow at the base of her throat, the erotic spot behind her ear. His nose nuzzled gently at her silken hair, inhaling the sweet scent.

She knew he intended to take his time arousing her, that he would leave no part of her untouched, unclaimed. That knowledge made her pulse quicken and her heart race. This would be no quick culmination of desire, but a slow savoring of pleasures eagerly anticipated.

As his fingers moved in sensuous circles on her shoulders, Devon trembled, then bit her lower lip to stop herself from crying out in wanton abandonment. The sweet ache she had felt since that unfulfilled erotic fantasy in the screening room filled her again. But this time, she knew, it would be sated.

His mouth was plunging into the hollow between her breasts now. With agonizing slowness his lips moved across her breasts. When he reached her erect nipple, he paused, then circled it slowly.

Wave after wave of the most unimaginable pleasure coursed through her body, making her writhe with an agony she hoped would never end.

He was relentless. As his lips explored her breasts, his hands stroked every curve of her quivering body. Inside her a coil was tightening now, demanding release. Her fingers were entwined in his golden hair as she unconsciously pulled him even closer.

As his lips moved down her body he murmured words of love and pleasure. His voice was thick with desire, the words barely audible. But she knew what he meant, and she responded with a moan of ecstasy.

His hands were gentle but insistent as they moved sensuously over her hips. When he parted her thighs, she gasped. When his lips descended across her stomach and lower, she gasped again.

But his mouth continued downward to her thigh. He placed teasingly light kisses along the length of her leg, on the inside of her knee, on the tender sole of her foot, before returning on a different path up the other leg.

His lips moved ever upward until she lay trembling, holding her breath expectantly. His searching tongue was indeed exploring every inch of her body, every curve and hollow, to the most intimate, hidden places.

"No," she gasped, suddenly nervous. But she meant yes and he knew it.

He went on. And then there was nothing but sweet oblivion as she arched against him, her body rigid with the most intense pleasure she had ever known. Her mouth opened in a silent scream, her eyes closed, and she felt she was drowning in a sea of ecstasy.

But the ending was just the beginning. When it was over and she lay completely relaxed, he moved up to nuzzle her neck once more.

"We've only just begun, sweetheart," he promised.

Her smoldering eyes opened to gaze adoringly into his. Her hands slipped up his strong, muscular arms to his shoulders. "Come here," she said softly.

He moved between her still-parted thighs and took her as gently as his rising passion would allow. She was eager for him. She arched against him, enveloping him in the warmth and intimacy of her body. The cleaving unto each other was a gift. She was transfixed with the wonder of it. Such intimacy seemed almost to transcend reality.

We will love like this for eternity, she thought.

Then all awareness was replaced by intense shock waves that made what she had felt earlier seem merely like ripples in a pond.

After a few moments he moved to lie beside her, not loosening his hold on her. She lay within his possessive arms, unwilling to move one inch. Her body was sated, her mind at peace. One hand lay on his arm; the other was pressed against his chest, feeling the strong beat of his heart.

In a low voice he talked to her, telling her of his thoughts and feelings as he made love to her. She responded with equal honesty, unwilling to fall asleep, to relinquish the intimacy of the time.

While one arm cradled her body close to his, the other lay across her breasts, his hand lightly stroking the side of her neck. Brushing back her tousled hair, he softly kissed her forehead.

Devon inhaled his special scent, his warmth enveloping her. Thoroughly at ease with him now, she allowed one finger to lazily trace the hard contours of the muscles on his chest.

Glancing down the entire length of her naked body, Spence let his gaze linger on her gently rounded breasts before lowering slowing to stare appreciatively at the curves and hollows of her waist, hips and thighs.

Devon felt a flicker of the desire that only minutes earlier had been completely sated. Unconsciously she moved closer to him, until the tips of her breasts barely touched his chest.

Spence's expression changed from satisfied laziness to smoldering desire. "How does this feel?" he asked, his thumb circling in a slow, erotic motion on her shoulder.

"Mmm, nice," she whispered.

As his hand moved down to her breast, his thumb still circling her sensitive skin seductively, he continued, "And this?"

He had reached a rose-tinted nipple now. It tautened voluptuously in response to his expert caress.

Devon said, "Oh, *yes . . .*" as her breath came erratically.

His lips lightly brushed hers, tantalizing her, before

moving down to the rigid nipple. Her senses were startled, then inflamed.

A soft whimper of bliss escaped Devon. Her hands moved to Spence's back, one hand clasping his nape, the other running over the hard planes from his shoulder blades to the small of his back.

He groaned as her fingers splayed over his firm buttocks.

"Tell me more about your fantasies," he urged in a husky whisper.

Devon hesitated. Then she began to speak to him, her words punctuated by soft caresses and tantalizing strokes.

Not until dawn bathed the dark rooftops of London in a golden glow did Devon and Spence finally fall asleep in each other's arms. As Devon's thick, sooty lashes closed over her eyes, she sighed softly.

As Spence had promised, all of her fantasies were fulfilled. As were his, she knew from the words he whispered to her just before she fell asleep.

Chapter 12

SPENCE SLOWLY OPENED HIS EYES. HE FOUND THE ROOM barely lit by thin, slanting light coming in through a narrow opening in the drapes. Next to him lay Devon, her tousled, silky hair a dark halo around her face. Propping himself up on one arm, he looked down at her peacefully sleeping form. He knew their vigorous night of lovemaking, on top of her killing work schedule, had exhausted her. She looked as if she would sleep for hours.

Silently he took this opportunity to look at her while she was unguarded, vulnerable. Her lashes were a dark fringe lying softly on her cheeks. Her turned-up nose might almost have been a child's. But her lips, especially that sensuous full lower one, were still a bit swollen from his ardent kisses. There was nothing of the child about them.

His glance lowered to her naked shoulders, visible above the sheet she clutched to her breast with one hand. Her skin was like the darkest honey, smooth, soft, enticing. He felt a stirring in his loins and knew if he remained in bed, he would want to take her again. But he didn't want to disturb this deep sleep she so obviously needed.

With infinite care he rose, barely disturbing the bed and making not a sound. He grabbed the clothes he'd left in a pile on the floor, then went downstairs. His careful tread on the carpeted floor barely disturbed the stillness of the room.

Downstairs in the sitting room, he turned on a light, for it was still rather dim in those first few hours after sunrise on a November London morning. He dressed quickly. Then, in case Devon awoke before he returned, he sat down at the desk and wrote a note to her.

"Good morning, sleepyhead. I'll be back soon with a surprise."

He signed it in his bold scrawl, then propped the paper against the lamp on the desk.

Ten minutes later he had returned to his own suite in the hotel, changed into jeans and a heavy white bulky knit sweater and was walking down Roland Gardens, the street that bisected Blakes Hotel. It was a glorious morning, cool, crisp and sunny. Even after only two hours' sleep he felt invigorated. Shoving his hands in his pockets, he strolled leisurely through Kensington, glorying in the beautiful scenery and his own marvelous mood.

It had been years since he'd felt this way— lighthearted, unpressured, as if all were right with the world. And he knew whom he had to thank for this.

Devon.

God! the very sound of her name was lovely.

As Spence passed the attractive squares and crescents of that exclusive residential section of London, he thought about the previous night. He'd never known it could be that way. Even with Tricia he hadn't felt that intimacy, that sharing, both physically and emotionally.

For once Spence had let down the guard he'd always felt was necessary for his survival.

When he had heard people talk about sex being a spiritual experience, he had been frankly cynical. It was pleasurable, certainly, but nothing more.

Now I know what they meant, he thought, shaking his head in amazement. When he and Devon made love, he felt for the first time in his adult life that he didn't have to be ultimately alone, that there could be a bonding more powerful than anything he'd ever dreamed of. When he and Devon were together . . .

He let the thought trail off pleasantly.

As Spence walked down the street, his face was lit by a perpetual half smile that made passersby pause and smile in return.

London is the most beautiful city in the world, he thought happily. Although, I'd probably say the same about Cleveland if I were there this morning.

Tossing back his head, he laughed out loud, totally unconcerned about how he looked.

He passed Regency houses brightly transformed into fashionable boutiques and restaurants. Finally he came to Kensington Gardens, acres in area, once the private gardens of Kensington Palace. He ambled down a beautiful avenue of trees. Passing between a lovely sunken garden and a group of bay and thorn trees, he suddenly saw the palace itself. He knew Charles and Diana, the Prince and Princess of Wales, lived there. He'd ignored their storybook wedding, convinced that their royal romance was a superficial fantasy that would soon disappear in the face of reality.

This morning he was much more prepared to believe that fairy tales could come true.

Glancing at his watch, he saw that it was past ten o'clock. Devon might be awakening soon. Hurriedly leaving the gardens, he flagged down a taxi and told the driver to take him to Fortnum and Mason.

In that luxurious department store the assistants in the grocery department wore black frock coats. Cornering one of them, Spence proceeded to tell him exactly what he wanted. Twenty minutes later he left with a wicker picnic basket filled with the famous store's most expensive delicacies.

As he sat in the backseat of the taxi, he thought about returning to Devon. They wouldn't have much time. They were returning to LA that afternoon. . . .

Suddenly his thoughts stopped. LA. The studio. Their night of lovemaking.

His thoughts were jumbled, but one thing was clear: This idyll was to be short-lived. Once they returned to LA, Devon would once more be the head of the studio and he would be someone she shouldn't be involved with.

For the first time all morning it occurred to Spence just how profoundly Devon had compromised herself. She might well wake up regretting what had happened between them. He remembered now how she had protested, but he had been blind to her protests.

Damn! he muttered under his breath. His euphoria was shattered.

Chapter 13

DEVON YAWNED AND STRETCHED LAZILY. AS HER SLEEP-fogged mind gradually became alert, she remembered where she was and what had happened the night before. Smiling that same satisfied smile Scarlett O'Hara had worn when she awoke after a night of lovemaking with Rhett Butler, she turned to look at Spence.

His side of the bed was rumpled but empty.

Looking at the clock beside the bed, Devon was amazed to see that it was nearly eleven. She was normally an early riser, but then, she realized with a rueful grin, this morning she'd been especially tired.

Lying back on the pillow, she sighed deeply. Her body had never felt this way before, a bit sore as if from a hard workout, yet thoroughly sated and deliciously relaxed.

Last night . . . it was every dream she'd ever had rolled into one. Facets of herself that she had not even been aware of had been revealed. Never before had she felt so free with a man. She'd given herself to Spence with complete abandon after that initial token resistance.

It had never been that way before. With Tony she'd always felt slightly insecure, aware that his interest in her might very well be transitory. There had been a feeling of emptiness that had remained unfilled. Until now. Until Spence.

She hadn't thought it possible that a man could touch her as he had done . . . as if she were at once the most fragile porcelain and the most cardinal flesh.

"Mmm . . ." she murmured aloud, drawing out the sound pleasurably.

She was wide awake now, curious about where Spence had gone. Rising, she slipped on a red silk jacquard caftan. Bias cut, with graceful lines, it would have been demurely modest were it not for the thigh-high slit on one side that revealed most of her long, slender leg.

In the bathroom she splashed water on her face to wake herself up thoroughly, then quickly ran a brush through her hair.

She was just descending the stairs to the sitting room when the door opened and Spence came in.

She paused, one hand on the stair rail, one foot slightly raised to descend to the next step. He looked up at her.

She had wondered what it would be like, this first meeting after their night of love. Would they be nervous, awkward with each other? Would she search for some sign of affection on Spence's face and find nothing but the blankness that follows meaningless sex? Now that her desire was sated, would she look at him and feel nothing?

None of those fears were realized. He looked at her

with such transparent delight that she knew the night had pleased him, touched him, as deeply as it had her. And as she quickly scanned his face, taking in the features she knew so well now, she felt again how very, very special their night together had been. She felt no awkwardness or disappointment. Nothing but a profound sense of the rightness of their being together.

"Hi," he said in a low voice. "Did you see my note?"

She shook her head, then admitted, "I only just got up."

"Well, I've brought breakfast. Or, I suppose I should say, brunch."

It was only then that she noticed the wicker basket in his hand. She'd been so caught up in staring at his face, she wasn't aware of anything else.

Closing the door behind him, he walked to the center of the sunlit room. She came down the stairs and joined him.

As he spread out a checkered blanket over the carpet, he explained, "Compliments of Fortnum and Mason. I wasn't sure what you'd like, so I got a bit of everything."

As he named the contents he set them out on the blanket. "Peaches in brandy. Caviar—Russian beluga —and the thinnest wheat crackers, or 'biscuits' as the very proper assistant referred to them. Champagne —Château Lafite Rothschild. Scones with lemon curd."

When she made a face, he smiled and said, "I know, it sounds awful. But it's delicious, sort of like lemon-flavored whipped cream." Then he continued to unpack. "Grapes. Hothouse strawberries with Devonshire cream. And for dessert . . ."—he pulled out a small box wrapped in shiny gold foil—"Godiva chocolates. Don't worry. I won't make you ride naked on a horse to eat them."

Devon knelt down beside him on the edge of the blanket. Opening the lid and looking over the luscious, delicately designed chocolates, she replied, "Mmm, for these I'd almost do it. How did you know I'm a chocoholic?"

"I don't know anyone who isn't."

He set out plates, silverware and two tall, elegant, blue-tinged glasses of Baccarat crystal. He poured champagne for them both, then they each heaped their plates with food. Before they began to eat, Devon raised her glass to him.

"A toast," she said.

He stopped, then raised his glass to hers.

"To the simple things in life," she finished slyly.

He threw back his head and laughed appreciatively. For the first time since he had come in a few minutes earlier, he seemed to relax. Then he touched his glass to hers. A sound, as clear and high as only the finest crystal can make, rang out.

For the next several minutes they devoted themselves to eating. Devon was ravenous. Everything was utterly delicious, and she thought she would never get enough of it. She spread the thick, creamy lemon curd on a soft scone, then bit into it. It was heavenly, incredibly rich and smooth. This was followed by a brandied peach, then caviar piled high on crackers. She dipped strawberries in the Devonshire cream, far richer and sweeter than any whipped cream she'd ever tasted.

Finally, though, as her appetite lessened, it occurred to her that Spence was silent. And he hadn't referred to the previous night at all.

Was my first impression wrong? she wondered suddenly in a burst of self-doubt. Does he feel about last night as I do, or was it just another Spencer Tait

one-night stand? Does he treat all his ladies so gallantly, just before he takes his leave?

Her appetite was gone entirely now. She looked at
him hopefully, willing him to say something, to reassure her that the intimacies they had shared went
beyond a superficial sexual attraction.

But he was silent. And thoughtful.

She wondered if he was trying to decide how to tell
her last night was both the beginning and the end.

Suddenly the telephone rang. The noise broke the
quiet intimacy of the moment. Devon rose reluctantly
and answered it. After saying, "Hello," she listened for
a moment, then replied, "No, don't come by. I'll meet
you at the plane."

After hanging up, she turned to Spence. "That was
my secretary. She was just reminding me that our plane
leaves in three hours."

He was silent for a moment longer. Then, as if finally
coming to a decision that he had put off as long as
possible, he rose and faced her. His face was a mask,
his eyes unreadable. Devon could see nothing there of
the man who had opened himself to her so completely
only a few brief hours earlier.

"Devon, I'm sorry about last night."

No! she thought desperately. Whatever you do, don't
apologize. Don't make what we shared something that
has to be apologized for.

But he continued, "I won't offer excuses. I'll just
assure you it won't happen again. We *do* have to work
together. . . ."

She stopped him in a voice so cold she hardly
recognized it as her own. "Exactly. We have to work
together. I have a studio to run and you have a film to
make for that studio."

Something flickered in his eyes, something almost
like pain. But Devon knew it couldn't be that. She

finished, "Now, if you don't mind, I have packing to do. I'll see you on the plane, I'm sure."

He nodded. And without saying another word, he strode out of the room.

Devon continued standing there, her body rigid, for several long seconds before the tears began to trickle down her cheeks.

Chapter 14

BACK IN LOS ANGELES BOTH DEVON AND SPENCE WENT about their work with renewed dedication. They rarely saw each other, and when they did, they were excruciatingly polite.

Devon told no one of their night together in London. She tried to put it out of her mind, but she couldn't. The memories were too vivid and insistent—and too painful.

As preproduction on *Last Chance* got well under way they found that they worked extremely well together. Each had qualities that complemented the other. Spence was a genius at the creative side of the business. He knew instinctively which actor would be best for each role, what the look and tone of the film should be. Devon knew how to handle the business end, the budget, the deal-making.

Devon always made sure that other people were present at her meetings with Spence—usually Sally and

Karl, and occasionally Terry Bernstein, the production manager. Thus, for a month, she managed never to be alone with him.

Then one evening as she was getting ready to leave, Marci gave her a message. The final cut of *Images* was about to be screened.

Devon hesitated. Then, as Marci stood waiting, she said, "You can leave now. I'll see you in the morning."

"Thanks, Miss O'Neill. Good night."

When Marci was gone, Devon still stood in the middle of her office.

Don't be ridiculous, she told herself. This is just part of the job. I can't very well *not* see the final cut of a movie we're going to be releasing shortly. I won't have to say more than a few words to Spence.

Grabbing her coat and purse, she headed down to the screening room in the basement, intending to go straight home afterward.

To her surprise, and discomfiture, Spence was alone in the room. As she walked in he looked a little shocked to see her.

"Oh . . . hi." His voice sounded unnaturally polite, as if he were talking to someone he didn't know very well. As if, Devon thought, he were talking to a mere acquaintance and not a woman he worked with. A woman he'd made love to.

She sat down, forcing herself to take the seat next to his. She wouldn't let him see how his nearness affected her.

"You can start now," he said into the intercom.

As the room dissolved into blackness, Devon asked, "Isn't anyone else coming?"

"No." He added, "Actually I was going to watch this alone. Then I thought I'd better let you in on it."

Devon's breath caught and for a moment she couldn't have spoken if she'd had to. What she had avoided for a long, miserable two weeks had finally happened. She was alone with the man whose very look could set her body on fire. She stared rigidly ahead at the screen, watching the familiar credits roll past to the accompaniment, now, of a lush, lyrical score.

Don't think about him being so near, she told herself with a growing sense of desperation. But it was impossible not to think about him when she could hear his breathing, smell his musky scent, feel his arms moving on the chair arm next to her.

And the movie only made it all worse. She'd found it tremendously sensual before. Now, in its finished state, with the music adding to the mood of sexual longing and fulfillment, it was powerfully affecting. As the love scenes unfolded they had an even more heady impact on her than they had had the first time she'd seen them. For now she didn't have to fantasize about what it would be like to make love to Spencer Tait. She knew.

Oh, God! She knew what his arms felt like when they enveloped her in their gentle strength, what his fingertips felt like when they traced a searing path along her quivering body, what his lips felt like when they possessed hers. . . .

She couldn't bear it. Tears stung the back of her eyes and there was a lump in her throat. She was only dimly aware of THE END flashing across the screen, of the lights coming on, of Spence saying into the intercom, "Thanks, Frank, you can go now."

She couldn't face him. It was weak, she knew, and she despised herself for it, but she couldn't do it. Without looking at him, she grabbed her purse and coat and nearly ran from the screening room.

Outside, the wide hallway was deserted. It was late, and everyone else had long since left.

"Devon!"

She stopped abruptly as if her body had been jerked

to a halt by a rope. Her breathing was erratic, her expression tortured as she turned slowly to face Spence.

The rigid politeness he'd shown earlier was gone. Instead he looked as tortured as she did.

"Devon," he repeated. This time it wasn't a command but a plea. In his voice was more anguish than she would ever have thought possible.

She walked as if by compulsion into his arms.

As she looked into those green eyes, she whispered, "Why did you apologize?"

He was startled. Then, the dawning of understanding lit his face. "I thought . . . oh, my darling Devon, I thought I'd forced something on you that you regretted."

She felt as if a heavy burden that had been weighing her down forever was suddenly lifted. He didn't regret what had happened. He simply thought she did.

"Oh, my foolish, foolish love," she whispered. But now her voice was light. The strain was gone.

He kissed her then, with all the pent-up passion of a month of frustration.

She thought she would melt, her body evaporate into the air, because at that moment of pure bliss she didn't feel at all real.

When he finally released her, he smiled at her, and her heart flip-flopped.

"What on earth are we to do?" she asked, keeping her arms around his neck, where they had gone automatically, as if of their own volition. There was no concern in her voice, though. Only curiosity.

He laughed, and she knew he shared her feeling of almost absurd happiness. "I honestly don't know. But one way or another, we've got to have some time together."

"I don't want it to be common knowledge. Not yet."

"I know."

"For a while, at least, let's try to keep it a secret."

Spence arched one blond eyebrow quizzically. "A secret in Hollywood? You know better than that, Devon. I know, you're concerned about your position . . ."

"It isn't just that. I don't want . . . oh, all the prying, the gossip, the stares when we're together."

"I understand, sweetheart."

The term of endearment, spoken so matter-of-factly, affected her profoundly. Her breath caught and it was a moment before she could speak. She knew a private romantic idyll couldn't go on forever. No secret lasts long in Hollywood. All she hoped for was a little time to get to know each other, to decide if their futures lay together, before going public.

"I have an idea," Spence said. With a devilish grin he said, "Las Brisas."

"But Acapulco . . ." Devon responded thoughtfully. "That's hardly an out-of-the-way place. We'd be bound to run into people who might recognize us."

"Not if we get a villa at Las Brisas and avoid the 'in' spots. We'll leave tomorrow night and come back Monday."

As Devon thought about the bleak winter day that was just ending, she realized how wonderful it would be to spend some time in that warm, sunny place, sipping margaritas. And making love to Spence.

"Okay," she agreed.

"I'll make the arrangements and we'll meet at the airport."

Devon felt as if she were setting out on an adventure, a journey to forbidden places. And she was, in a way, she knew.

Late the following night, Friday, they arrived at Las Brisas, one of the most elegant hotels in Acapulco. Overlooking the city's lovely bay, it featured private villas, each with its own swimming pool. It provided both privacy and an unabashedly romantic atmosphere.

Devon and Spence arrived at the drive-in reception lounge and were immediately given tequila coolers. A cool breeze blew in off the bay, which sparkled silver where moonlight lit a wide swath across it.

As the manager led them to their *casita*, he explained, "This is our twenty-fifth anniversary. The bands in the bars and restaurants are playing music of the 1950's, and tomorrow night there will be a 'pink and white' dance. Champagne cocktails will be served— compliments of the hotel, of course," he added with a friendly smile.

Spence grinned. "I'll lose myself in nostalgia. I hope they play 'Blue Suede Shoes.' Turning to Devon, he finished slyly, "Maybe I should grease my hair and buy a beat-up leather jacket."

"If you do, I'll cut my hair in a duck tail and wear a poodle skirt."

Looking at her with profound warmth in his eyes, he said, "I wish I'd known you then. When you were hardly more than a little girl."

"I wish I'd known you forever," Devon responded, her voice suddenly thick with desire.

The manager coughed politely to get their attention. Looking at him, Devon found him watching them with amused tolerance. The expression on his dark, jovial face seemed to say, "Lovers, of course. We get a lot of those here."

He opened the door to the *casita*, and the bellboy carried their luggage inside. It was a small, opulently furnished villa. The manager pointed out a refrigerator stocked with platters of fresh fruit, soft drinks and a bar filled with liquor.

"Oh, it's lovely!" Devon exclaimed.

"Have you been here before, *señorita, señor?*" he asked.

"No," both Devon and Spence answered at once.

"Then let me explain. Room-service waiters will bring hot rolls and coffee in the morning at whatever time you wish so that breakfast will be ready when you awake. The hotel has its own seaside beach club, La Concha, which is exclusively for members of the hotel. If I may be of service in any way, please do not hesitate to ask. I want your stay with us to be a memorable one."

Glancing at Spence, Devon thought it would most certainly be that.

When the manager and the bellboy left, Spence suggested they go to one of the numerous bars for a drink.

"Great, but let me change," Devon replied. She had dressed in a white linen pantsuit for the plane trip. Now, she opened her suitcase and quickly changed into a soft silk jacquard blouse, which was gathered at the neck and had billowing poet sleeves, and a matching dirndl skirt.

Spence was wearing tan slacks and a blazer with an emerald-green silk shirt that nearly matched his eyes. He felt no need to change, and as soon as she was ready, they went out into the starlit night.

At the bar a waitress took their order for margaritas after seating them at a small secluded table. "What a wonderful idea this was," Devon said, smiling across the small candlelit table at Spence.

"I have lots of wonderful ideas," he teased. "And I'll be happy to enumerate them for you . . . or better still, I'll be happy to demonstrate them for you."

"Later," Devon said with a delighted laugh.

As they sipped their drinks they listened to a small combo play old and familiar tunes. Then the group began to play an old Elvis Presley song, "Are You Lonesome Tonight?"

"Want to dance?" Spence asked softly.

Devon nodded. They walked out onto the small dance floor, where a handful of other couples were dancing, and he took her in his arms. Devon closed her eyes and laid her head on his shoulder. Relaxing completely, her body melding perfectly with his, she put herself in his hands.

She had been only twelve when the 1950's ended. But she could remember going to her first school dances that year, sock hops in the gym during the lunch hour and a special Christmas dance. Remembering herself at twelve, just budding into young womanhood, she smiled indulgently.

How awkward I felt at those dances, she thought. I was taller than most of the boys. The awful suspense of standing there, waiting for someone to ask me to dance, wondering if the very worst would happen—if no one at all would approach me.

She sighed softly.

"What is it, sweetheart?" Spence asked, whispering in her ear.

She looked up at him. Smiling shyly, she admitted, "I was just remembering the pain of adolescence. Junior high dances."

He smiled in understanding. "I've never been so scared in my life as when I asked a girl to dance for the very first time," he admitted.

"I never thought about it from that viewpoint. I just knew it was absolute agony, waiting to be asked."

"I can't believe the boys in your school were foolish enough to overlook you."

"For a while they were. Then by the Christmas dance I didn't have to worry because I had a boyfriend."

Spence raised one blond eyebrow quizzically. "Oh? And who was this teen-age Lothario?"

Devon laughed lightly. "Steven Madrid. He had black hair and flashing dark eyes, and he was absolutely

the handsomest boy in school. All the girls were crazy
about him, and when I walked into the Christmas dance
with him, I swear there was no one in the world I
envied."

Remembering that moment of triumph, Devon's face
softened and her expression grew far-away and
dreamy.

I remember that night so vividly, she thought. Even
now I can remember exactly how happy I felt. Why is
that?

And then she knew. Because two days later her
father had died. The night of the Christmas dance was
the last happy time she had known before the tragedy
of losing her father.

"What's wrong?" Spence asked worriedly.

Devon realized her expression must have grown sad,
for he was looking at her with real concern in his eyes.
When she explained what had happened, he was silent
for a moment. Then he said in a voice so low she could
barely hear him, though he was only inches from her,
"The day my mother died, I was playing Monopoly
with some friends. We were laughing, drinking Cokes,
ruthlessly trying to ruin each other financially. That
money might almost have been real, the way we were
trying to accumulate it all."

He paused, and for a moment Devon heard the
music clearly: *Are you lonesome tonight? Do you miss
me tonight?*

Then Spence continued in a voice that was only
barely under control, "My uncle called me at my
friend's house to tell me my father was at the hospital
with my mother. The hospital was only two blocks
away. I ran, but it was too late.

"That was the last time I played that game," he said
finally.

For a moment Spence's green eyes met Devon's blue

ones. They were open, vulnerable, revealing such pain that Devon wanted to hold him like a baby in her arms and croon to him, "It's all right, it's all right."

Then the song ended.

As they stood there, no longer moving, Devon reached up to cup his face in both her hands. "I love you, you know," she said softly.

"I know," he replied. "Let me love you in return."

He led her off the dance floor and back to their villa.

A fire burned in the adobe fireplace, the embers glowing golden red in the darkness. Devon and Spence lay naked on the huge bed. As he pressed his body against hers she felt exquisite sensations as her taut, rosebud nipples were crushed against the smooth, hard skin of his broad chest.

Her hips pushed against his, and she felt a hard, throbbing pressure between her legs. Slowly she slipped her leg between his, her arms pulling him toward her as if she couldn't get close enough to him.

A groan escaped his lips before he brought them down on hers, plundering her mouth.

His hands were all over her, exploring the secret places they'd come to know so intimately that night in London. As his fingers ran lightly over her abdomen, finally reaching the soft, curling tendrils, it was as if her body, asleep for a long time, was being gently awakened.

Her back arched at his touch; her breathing grew fast. While his fingers probed between her legs, gently prying them apart, his lips brushed her cheek, the length of her slender neck, the hollow between her full breasts. His tongue circled her nipples, making them grow even harder.

He pushed her down on the bed, and for a tantalizing second his body hovered over her. Then they were joined and the gentle rocking motion began. Her body moved perfectly with his. As the movement grew faster, more urgent, her nails dug into his back. She tried to pull him even closer, to become part of him.

His lips were on hers, his tongue probing the warm moistness of her mouth, while his hands pulled her hips up to meet his.

And then came the fire, a spark at first. It grew quickly, igniting her, making her body as taut as a bowstring stretched to the breaking point. But the sensation didn't break; it continued. Wave after wave of fire spread through her rigid body. . . .

When Devon awoke in the morning, Spence was still asleep. He lay against her, one arm over her shoulder. He'd made love almost desperately to her the night before, taking her again and again, until they were both exhausted. She knew that talking about his mother's death had been a catharsis for him. Somehow she felt sure he'd never done it before. Making love to her, joining with her to defeat the awful loneliness that she sensed was at the core of his personality, was part of that catharsis.

And he'd said "I love you." She smiled now at the memory.

Watching him sleep, she thought how boyish he looked. The lines of worry that creased his forehead when he was dealing with the business of filmmaking were smoothed out. The mouth that could tighten with anger at setbacks or incompetence was relaxed.

One lock of wheat-colored hair fell across a closed eyelid. Reaching over, she tenderly brushed it back. Then, with infinite care, she moved his arm so that she could rise. Without disturbing him, she slipped from the bed. Taking a burgundy-colored terry robe from the closet, she wrapped it around her, tying the belt loosely, then stepped outside onto the patio that surrounded the pool.

Hibiscus petals floated on the serene blue water. Devon knew a maid must have brought them earlier while she and Spence slept. Walking up to the white adobe wall, which was waist-high, she looked out at the view.

This morning the sun shone brilliantly over the breathtaking sweep of bay. Mountains surrounded the luxury hotels, which stood side by side on the bay. Perfect white beaches formed a crescent around the deep blue water. It was like a scene from the garden of Eden, the dazzling sunlight, richly colorful flowers spilling over the walls of the surrounding villas and climbing the terraced hillside.

Hundreds of yards below she saw the La Concha beach club where guests were already swimming in the saltwater pools while mobile bars swung around the perimeter, dispensing margaritas and piña coladas.

Suddenly strong arms encircled her waist. A deeply masculine voice, still thick with sleep, said, "Good morning, Eve."

Laughing, Devon turned to face Spence. He hadn't bothered with a robe. In their secluded villa she knew no one could see them. Only habit had prompted her to put on her own.

"Good morning, Adam," she replied with a grin, and slipped her arms around his neck.

"How about a swim, then breakfast?" he suggested lazily.

"Mmm, sounds marvelous. I'll change."

"Don't bother." He pulled at her sash-belt and the robe came open. In an instant he had slipped it off her shoulders, and they stood naked together. Her olive skin was dark against his golden tan.

"I'll help you in," he teased, picking her up.

"Spencer Tait, don't you dare throw me in!" she shrieked before he dropped her unceremoniously in the warm, clear water. As she rose to the top, brushing back her wet hair, she saw him execute a perfect dive into the pool, his lean body slicing the water cleanly.

He came up a few feet from her, and she immediately splashed him playfully. For half an hour they played like children, laughing, teasing. The water was an incredibly sensuous environment as their bare skin touched, slid, melded.

Finally they stepped out of the pool. After drying off, Spence pulled on brief white shorts and a tank top that revealed a great deal of his broad, hard chest. Devon put on a mauve caftan.

He brought in the breakfast tray that had been left outside their door only minutes earlier, while she got a tray of fruit out of the small refrigerator. They set the food on the table on the patio.

"What shall we do today?" he asked a few minutes later, as he sipped his second cup of coffee. "Swim at the beach club? Go on a safari into the jungle? Wander around the town square?"

"Let's do it all," Devon responded eagerly. "I've never been here before. I don't want to miss anything."

"If we run into anyone we know, we'll simply say we're here on business," Spence reassured her.

"Oh, I don't even care," Devon replied. "Now that we're here, I just want to enjoy it to the fullest. I'm not going to worry about gossip-mongers."

"Good for you!" Setting down his cup, Spence said, "Let's get to it, then. We've got a lot to do."

After dressing, they took one of the Jeeps provided by the hotel and drove down to the town. They wandered through the quaint shops of the *zocalo*, the town square, and admired the cathedral with its big blue spires.

Then they went on a safari organized by the hotel. It was far from the simple excursion Devon had anticipated. There was a mobile bar and musicians to play romantic melodies as the caravan swung into a coconut plantation at Cayaco. Next the motorcade moved on to a secluded beach for a picnic and burro races. They took a canoe ride up a jungle river. Streams ran from the jungle to the sea, and beside the streams women did their laundry, leaving it to dry on the rocks. Naked children played happily beside their hardworking mothers.

Watching the giggling, splashing children, Spence turned to Devon, sitting beside him in the canoe, and asked, "Do you want kids?"

She hesitated. This was a serious subject for her, and she had no idea how Spence felt about it. Finally she replied, "I want children very badly. As I grow older, the urge gets stronger. But my biological clock is running out. This Christmas I'll be thirty-five. I can't wait much longer."

"I want children too. I didn't when I was younger. But now . . . I don't think my life would be really meaningful without having a child."

Devon was thoughtful for a long moment. Then she said, "I have a problem—maybe an insurmountable one. I don't want governesses to raise my children. My father worked at home, so even when my mother was away on a film, he was there. I was never left with servants. I want to give my children that kind of commitment. But I also want to continue my career.

"I want to make good films," she concluded. "And I want to have children. But we can't always have everything we want."

Looking at Spence, she asked, "What do you want?"

He didn't hesitate. "I want to own my own films. I want to control them, from beginning to end, from the writing of the script to the distribution of the finished film. I want to be the one to decide what to do with what I make."

"You have less interference than most filmmakers because of your success."

"Yes. But there's still interference. It's the studio that ultimately decides on the advertising campaign, the marketing strategy. I have to get the studio president's okay—*your* okay—to get financing for a film."

He softened his words with a wry smile, but once more Devon was reminded of the awkwardness of their positions.

Even in paradise, she thought dryly . . .

"I want the freedom to follow my own vision completely without dealing with Harrison Kahn and his board of directors, none of whom know anything about filmmaking."

"No filmmaker has that freedom. Even Francis Coppola couldn't manage it," Devon pointed out.

"There's no reason why I shouldn't try for it. That's why I'm doing this coventure deal on *Last Chance*. It's the first step toward my goal."

"Do you honestly think you'll ever achieve it?"

"I don't know. But I have to try. Even if I run the risk of losing everything. Because if I don't try for it, I've lost anyway. You can't be an artist and be safe."

Devon said nothing, but she knew exactly what he meant. She had her own dream that had once seemed almost impossible. And she'd achieved it.

When they returned to the hotel that evening, the lights of Acapulco twinkled around the bay. Spence changed into a tuxedo while Devon put on a white cashmere tunic sweater and long skirt, wrapped at the hip with a matching scarf, all studded with gold and silver nailheads. It was cool at night by the ocean, and she slipped a silver shawl over her shoulders as they left the villa.

They went to a restaurant where they could watch the famous high-divers jump from a tiny ledge into the surf of La Quebrada, hundreds of feet below. The gorge was lit with floodlights, and after each dive the divers climbed up the rocks, dripping and smiling, gathering gifts from the onlookers.

Spence ate enchiladas covered with sour cream and filled with tender crabmeat, while Devon had succulent shrimp in a spicy sauce. They sipped margaritas and they talked. Devon felt as if she could tell him everything, could talk to him forever without running out of things to say.

When they returned to the hotel late that night, Devon thought wistfully, I don't want to go home tomorrow. I don't want this fantasy to end.

But she knew it must.

Chapter 15

JUST BEFORE CHRISTMAS, SHEILA CALLED DEVON AT work.

"I just wanted to tell you I'm leaving today to fly up to the ranch," she said brightly. She was referring to her parents' ranch nestled in the foothills of the Sierra Nevada Mountains in Central California. "Will you be up as usual on Christmas Eve?"

Devon hesitated. The time had come to tell her mother about Spence. Somehow she felt awkward about it. Taking a deep breath, she forged ahead. "I'm going to be busy Christmas Eve, but I'll drive up on Christmas day."

"Oh."

"I'll be bringing someone with me," Devon continued.

"I *knew* it!" Sheila exclaimed. "You've had that cat-who-ate-the-canary look for the past two weeks. I must say, darling, I'm glad Spence doesn't mind spending his first Christmas with you, surrounded by your family. Some men might balk at that."

"Mother! How did you know it's Spence?"

"I know *you*, dear. With one unfortunate exception you've always had excellent taste in men. And from what I could tell from our brief meeting, Spencer Tait is the best catch in town."

Devon laughed. "You're amazing."

"Of course. You didn't get *all* your intelligence from your clever father. Now then, what time will you two be arriving?"

"We'll leave early so that we can be there by noon. I thought we'd spend the day, then drive back after dinner. We've both got an awful lot of work to do."

"I understand. Shooting will start soon on *Last Chance*, won't it?"

"Yes, in a little over a week."

"Well, I've got to run, Devon. Your grandfather sent his private plane and it's waiting for me at Palm Springs Airport right now. I'm late, as usual. I'll look forward to seeing both you and Spence on Christmas."

"'Bye, Mother."

After hanging up, Devon sat at her desk for a moment, thinking about her mother. She really was amazing.

Then she buzzed Marci to tell her she was leaving early to do some Christmas shopping. She really couldn't afford to take the time from her busy schedule, but if she didn't do it then, it would never get done.

A half hour later she was making her way through the crowds on Rodeo Drive. There was no snow on the ground, and the sun was shining brightly, but the exclusive shops had managed to create a festive Christmas atmosphere anyway. Windows were gaily decorated and the street itself was hung with lovely blue decorations and lights. Shoppers bustled past Devon, their arms laden with extravagantly wrapped packages.

Devon already had the presents for her family. She just needed to find something for Spence. But she had absolutely no idea what to get him. She wanted it to be very special, very personal. It wasn't simply a question of spending a lot of money on something impressive. This would be the first thing she had ever given him, and she wanted it to be something he would always cherish.

The problem wasn't that he already had everything. It was that he wanted so little. He didn't care about possessions, and his personal life-style was simple almost to the point of being Spartan. He dressed well when it was required, but otherwise wore casual, comfortable clothes.

As far as Devon knew, the only thing he really wanted was complete artistic freedom. Even though she was president of a studio, she couldn't give him that.

She sighed, frustrated, as she left yet another men's store empty-handed. It was five o'clock and the crowds were getting worse as people got off work and headed for the stores for last-minute shopping.

Stopping to glance in a jewelry store window, Devon considered a gold and platinum watch. The tiny, discreet price tag revealed that it was a steal at $12,000. It was one of the less expensive items in the window.

Not Spence's style, Devon decided, shaking her head and walking on. As she passed other windows she considered and rejected a cashmere sweater, a $1,100 bottle of Reserve du Fondateur cognac, a suede briefcase by Louis Vuitton, a crystal brandy decanter, a bronze horse statuette by Vanderveen, and a lovely etching of a Hopi Indian girl.

What do you get a man who spends his considerable income not on himself but on the movies he makes? she asked herself for the hundredth time. A man who buys caviar and brandied peaches for a picnic? And who prefers Levi's jeans, the older and more faded the better?

Then, just as she was about to give up in frustration and go home, she saw it.

What do you give a man who knows the safest way to hop a freight? Devon thought, grinning broadly.

A train.

The miniature Branch Line Freight Train set included the engine, coal car, three assorted cars, and a cherry-red caboose. It ran on a circular track in the window of a toy store. Devon stood there transfixed, happily watching it go around and around. It appealed to the child in her, and she felt certain somehow that it would also appeal to Spence.

Inside, Devon asked a young clerk to show her the train.

"For your little boy?" he asked.

Devon grew embarrassed. "Well . . . not exactly."

The young man smiled knowingly. "For an *older* boy?"

Devon nodded.

"Lucky guy," the clerk said. "My wife always gets me ties."

He went on to show Devon the train, which, though relatively small, had a great deal of track and many accessories—a tunnel, a bridge, a station and an intricate system of switches.

"Can you deliver it?" Devon asked. "And set it up? It would take me forever to put it together by myself."

"Of course." His tone indicated that stores on Rodeo Drive were *supposed* to cater to their customers.

As Devon left she felt more than a little silly. But Christmas is a time to be whimsical, she told herself. She hoped Spence would enjoy this bit of whimsy.

By five o'clock Christmas Eve the train was set up around the Christmas tree in Devon's living room.

Spence was due any minute, and Devon kept glancing out the window impatiently.

She had dressed casually but elegantly, in white satin hostess pajamas that emphasized her dark coloring. Her hair was loose, framing her face in soft waves and lightly brushing her shoulders.

On the coffee table was a bottle of wine and a plate of hors d'oeuvres. In the kitchen a crab quiche was cooling. That and a crisp green salad would be their dinner. For dessert she had made an incredibly rich chocolate mousse.

She had worked hard to make everything absolutely perfect for this first Christmas with Spence. She hoped it was only the first of many Christmases together.

She heard his firm tread on the walk outside. Before he had a chance to ring the doorbell, she opened the door and smiled at him warmly.

He had brought a suitcase, for he would be spending the weekend with her. Setting down the suitcase on the floor in the entryway, he took her into his arms and kissed her deeply.

"Merry Christmas," he said huskily, his eyes full of love.

"Merry Christmas," she replied. Then she continued, "Before you go into the living room, I have to explain something. I'm giving you your gift tonight."

"Oh? You mean I don't have to wait until the crack of dawn?" Spence responded, grinning happily.

"You see, it's something that I just couldn't wrap. There's no way to keep it a secret until tomorrow morning."

"This I've got to see."

She led him into the living room. She felt very awkward now, and shy, worried about how her gift would be received. Would he think it merely silly? Would he understand the love that was behind the thought?

Devon had selected a particularly large tree that especially happy Christmas. And she had decorated it with white doves and red velvet bows. At the top of the tree a silver and gold angel looked down beatifically. At the bottom ran the train track, circling the spreading green branches.

For a moment Spence simply stood stock still. Stunned surprise was his only expression.

He doesn't like it, Devon thought miserably. He thinks it's stupid.

Then he moved. Walking across the floor, he stopped at the black engine and bent down to touch it. Reaching out one finger, he pushed a tiny button that blew a shrill whistle. When he looked up at Devon, his eyes were shining brightly and his expression was joyous.

"Don't you want to help pull the switches?" he asked, grinning.

Devon's face broke into an ecstatic smile. "Oh, yes!"

Kneeling down on the floor next to him, she began to explain the operation of the train.

"Hold it, woman," Spence interrupted her with mock firmness. "You know how to run a studio, but *I* know about trains. You may pull the switches when I tell you, and if you're very good, I'll let you raise the bridge."

"Yes, sir," Devon replied meekly.

For the next hour they sipped the wine, nibbled on the hors d'oeuvres, and played with the train like a couple of kids.

Watching Spence, Devon knew her gift was more than a success. It had touched him deeply in a place where he hadn't allowed himself to be touched in a very long time.

At one point Spence looked across the train at Devon and said softly, "You've taken all the bah and humbug out of my Christmas. Thank you, sweetheart."

Devon smiled back at him, all the love in her heart visible in her eyes.

Finally, she suggested they eat. "Everything's ready. I'll just put it on the table," she said, while Spence continued to play with the train.

Five minutes later the dining room table was set with Spode china in a Christmas tree pattern. The quiche, salad, crusty French bread, and a bottle of Montrachet were in the center of the polished oak table.

"Spence, it's ready," she called over to him.

"Come here for just a minute," he responded.

When Devon reached him, she saw that the train was behind the tree.

"Since tomorrow's your birthday, I'll give you that present then. But because you gave me my Christmas present tonight, it's only fair I do the same for you."

Pushing a button, he started the train. As it came around the tree into full sight, Devon saw that a tiny package wrapped in silver foil sat in the coal car. Spence stopped the train in front of Devon.

Kneeling down, she picked up the small package and opened it carefully. It was one ounce of Joy, the most expensive perfume in the world, in a bottle of Baccarat crystal.

It was as meaningful, in its way, as her gift to him. For she knew that wherever she put it on her body, Spence would enjoy it. It was a tribute to the very special intimacy they shared.

"Thank you," she whispered, her voice suddenly thick with desire.

"You deserve it. You've been an awfully good little girl this year," he replied slyly. "Now, we'd better eat, because if you look at me that way much longer, I'll forget about dinner entirely."

Devon grinned. "Oh, no, you won't. Not after I spent half a day cooking!"

Laughing, he helped her to her feet, then they had the dinner that Devon had prepared so lovingly. Though they enjoyed it, neither of them could entirely concentrate on the food. Long before the Montrachet was gone, they had left the table and retired to the bedroom.

They awoke early the next morning. Turning to Spence, Devon smiled lovingly. "Good morning."

"Good morning yourself," he replied, leaning over to kiss her forehead and the tip of her nose.

"I'll make breakfast."

"*I'll* make breakfast while you get ready," he corrected her. "I know you're anxious to get started."

"Are you sure you don't mind going up to my grandparents' house?" Devon asked, not for the first time.

"As I've said before, no, I don't mind. I'm looking forward to it, in fact. I'll enjoy seeing your mother again." He patted Devon's bare derriere beneath the sheet. "Now, get going."

Devon smiled happily. "Okay. There are croissants and fresh fruit in the refrigerator."

Rising, Devon took a lavender robe of panne velvet from her closet and wrapped it around her body, which still carried a trace of Spence's scent. He slipped on a white terry robe from his suitcase and left the bedroom.

In the bathroom Devon filled the sunken tub with steaming hot water. She pulled her hair back in a ponytail, took off the robe, then sank into the tub.

The bathroom had been remodeled along with the bedroom. It was like a sunroom, filled with lush plants and wicker furnishings. The terra-cotta floor had thick white rugs scattered over it, and above the sunken tub was a stained-glass skylight. The tub was on a raised platform, with two terra-cotta steps leading up to it. An interesting collection of baskets held towels, soaps and lotions. Indirect lighting and a stereo system made it a room Devon could relax in.

But that morning Devon didn't have time to thoroughly relax. It was already seven-thirty and she wanted to leave by eight o'clock. After a quick bath she wrapped a giant yellow bathsheet around her glistening body, then sat down at the vanity in her bedroom and applied makeup. She brushed her hair out, leaving it loose. She had just put on a white mohair sweater over herringbone slacks when Spence returned with a breakfast tray. There were juice, coffee, warm croissants and fresh fruit. He set the tray down on a small round table near the tall window that overlooked the garden.

They ate quickly, for it was getting late, then started the drive up to the San Joaquin Valley. Devon knew it would be colder up there than in LA, so she brought a white wool greatcoat.

Spence had dressed with greater care than usual, in a tweed blazer that fit his broad shoulders snugly, a chocolate brown turtleneck sweater and matching slacks. Devon was aware that he wanted to make a good impression on her family, and she was touched by his effort.

They drove for four hours in Spence's Jaguar through the barren Tehachapi Mountains and into the San Joaquin Valley. Normally the valley was fog-enshrouded at that time of year, but that day it was sunny and crystal clear. The huge valley stretched northward as far as the eye could see, a patchwork quilt of varicolored fields, orchards and vineyards. To the right the majestic Sierra Nevadas were covered with pristine white snow.

"I've never been up here before," Spence said. "It's beautiful."

"Yes, in the winter it's gorgeous. In the summer it's

hot and brown and dry. But I love it. As a child, I spent a lot of time here on my grandparents' ranch. It was a world apart from Beverly Hills and Hollywood."

"It certainly is. I'll bet it's a hell of a lot better here."

"In some ways," Devon agreed. "Some day I'd like to have a small ranch here. Nothing like my grandparents', of course. They own two thousand acres. Just a small place to get away to sometimes when the business gets to be too much."

Spence flashed her a quick look of understanding. "That's why I moved to Malibu. I thought I'd get away from a lot of the Hollywood craziness. But Malibu isn't far enough."

"Oh, turn here," Devon said suddenly, indicating the next highway exit. Soon they were passing through the small town of Lemon Cove and were in the gently rolling foothills of the Sierra Nevadas.

They traveled for several miles down a narrow paved road and finally came in sight of Devon's grandparents' ranch. The house sat on the crest of a low hill overlooking the valley below. Save for a small area immediately around the house, the land was covered by orange groves.

The house was white, two stories, simple in the way of a country home. But it was no small farmer's place but the home of a big landowner.

When they drove up the circular drive in front of the house, the front door opened and Sheila came out. Devon ran up to her and they hugged warmly. As Spence walked up to them Sheila flashed her most beguiling smile and said, "Welcome, Spence. I hope I may call you that?"

"Of course. It's a pleasure to see you again, Mrs. O'Neill."

"Please call me Sheila. Now, come in and meet the family."

Devon had explained to Spence that Christmas was

the one time of the year when her far-flung relatives all got together. And they were all there today: Sheila's older brother and two younger sisters, with their families. The large house seemed full to overflowing with scampering children and happily chatting adults.

Sheila made quick, informal introductions, then left Spence with her parents while she and Devon passed out Devon's presents to her relatives.

Hank and Maryanne Lindsay were in their late seventies, but Hank still stood ramrod straight, and Maryanne's fine-boned face indicated where Sheila and Devon had gotten their beauty.

"So you're from Texas too," Hank began cordially.

From there the conversation centered almost entirely on differences between Galveston, Spence's hometown, and Dallas, Hank's.

As she helped her small cousins open their presents Devon glanced anxiously over at Spence, talking in a corner with her grandparents. She was relieved to see that he seemed to be enjoying himself. As she caught scraps of conversation she was amused to discover that he and her grandfather were talking like two good ol' boys, about oil, cattle, land and ranching in general. It was clear that Spence was happy to be talking about something other than the movies for a change.

Later in the afternoon, when the women were busy in the kitchen preparing the big Christmas dinner and the men were in the living room discussing the state of agriculture, Spence and Devon went for a walk.

"I like your family," he said sincerely.

"What's nice is that they're all so different. Aunt Katharine is a housewife and loves it. My mother was a movie star. Uncle Ronald works with grandfather and will take over the ranch someday. One cousin is a doctor, another is a model and one sells homemade cookies in Santa Cruz."

Spence grinned. "All in all, the typical American family." Then, growing more serious, he added, "You're lucky."

"I know."

They had walked across the broad expanse of lawn at the rear of the house and stopped at a whitewashed corral. Devon leaned on the railing and looked at a mare who was heavy with foal.

Spence's expression had grown sad, and there was a distant look in his eyes.

"I'm sorry," Devon said with infinite tenderness in her voice.

"For what?" he asked, his tone harsh.

"For everything you missed," she answered, not responding to the anger in his tone.

He hesitated, then his face softened and he gathered her in his arms. "I love you so much. The more I get to know you, the more I love you."

She nestled her head on his shoulder and circled his waist with her arms. She loved the feel of him, the strength tempered by tenderness. At that moment she felt overcome with happiness.

"We have to talk, Devon," he said. There was something in his voice, something that had never been there before.

She tensed and pulled away.

"Look at me," he commanded.

Reluctantly she did so. What she saw in his eyes made her feel weak with love for him.

"We both know this isn't just another affair," he said. "We've known it from the very beginning, but we didn't want to face it. The only question is—what are we going to do about it?"

She knew what he was getting at. Marriage. But it wasn't a simple matter of going through a ceremony and changing her name to Tait. They couldn't both continue working at UFS together. Even if Harrison would allow it, the hard truth was that Spence resented working under her. That wasn't a situation that could continue indefinitely without having an effect on their feelings for one another.

If Spence left, Harrison would be furious. If Devon left, giving up what she had worked so hard and so long for, she would feel resentful. Spence meant much more to her than her job. She knew that without a doubt. But her job mattered too. And if she had to give it up for him, that would always taint what she felt for him.

Damn! she thought. We can't even talk about marriage the way other people do. It has to be complicated, a case of one person losing in order for the other one to win.

Before he could say anything more, she said, "Let's not talk about it now. Let's wait until . . . until *Last Chance* is behind us."

His chin was set in a stubborn attitude that she'd come to know. She was afraid he was going to insist that a decision be made now.

He said nothing for a long moment. Finally he responded. "Okay. I understand the problems, Devon, and I can't honestly say I have any answers right now. So we'll wait. But not for long."

She knew that was a reluctant concession to her inner turmoil, and she appreciated it deeply. As they walked back to the house she told herself that all that mattered was the moment. The future, somehow, would take care of itself.

After a sumptuous dinner that night, there was a birthday cake for Devon. She opened her myriad presents, exclaiming happily over a suede jacket from her mother. But there was nothing from Spence. Her curiosity grew as to what he would give her and when. Finally, about nine o'clock, she and Spence took their leave.

"I'll call you next week," Sheila told Devon as she kissed her good-bye.

"Yes. And come by the studio. We'll have lunch again."

"All right, darling. Have a safe trip home." Turning to Spence, she added, "I'm so glad you could come."

"Thank you for having me. And for making me feel so welcome," he responded warmly.

They had left the narrow country road, passed through the town and were back on the highway when Spence said quietly, "Your present's in the glove compartment."

Devon grinned. "I was wondering when you were going to give it to me."

Excitedly she opened the glove compartment. Inside was a long, narrow package wrapped in shiny gold paper and tied with a gold velvet ribbon.

Opening it, Devon found a thin gold chain. Dangling from it was a single huge sapphire, stunning in its blue intensity.

"I noticed you prefer simple jewelry," Spence explained, keeping his eyes on the road. "I chose that because it's almost as blue as your eyes."

She felt more than sheer delight at his gift. Her heart swelled with love. "You almost make turning thirty-five a pleasure," she responded softly, reaching over to kiss his cheek.

"I'd like to see you wear it when we get back. That—and nothing else."

He put his arm around her and pulled her against him. They rode that way, in contented silence, much of the way to Los Angeles.

Chapter 16

On Monday morning Devon was back at work. Reluctantly she put behind her the special happiness of Christmas and concentrated on *Last Chance*. Rebecca, who was handling the contract negotiations, and Sally came in together.

"You've got to reign her in, Dev," Sally said, only half-jokingly. "She's low-balling all the people I want to hire."

"The industry's in a severe recession," Rebecca pointed out. "Everyone's looking for work. We don't have to pay outrageous salaries."

Sally grimaced. Devon smiled at her, then said to Rebecca, "Give me a rundown on how it's shaping up."

A half hour later Rebecca closed her notebook with a thoroughly satisfied expression on her face.

"Harrison will love you," Devon said, shaking her head in amazement at the low figures Rebecca had managed to negotiate. "Overall I agree with what you're doing. We've got to keep the costs down on this project. But I don't want to lose the key people over a dispute about a relatively small amount of money."

"Okay," Rebecca agreed. "I'll give in at the last minute, rather than let anyone get away."

"By the way, did you two have nice Christmases?" Devon asked.

"Great. I went skiing in Aspen," Rebecca answered.

"I *worked*," Sally answered ruefully. "The price of success, I guess."

"We don't have to ask how your Christmas was. You look thoroughly rested and happy," Rebecca observed.

Devon smiled, remembering.

"You want to tell us about Spence?" Rebecca continued matter-of-factly.

Devon's smile evaporated as she came back to earth with a thud. "How did you guess? Does anyone else know?"

Sally quickly calmed her anxiety. "Nobody but us." She flashed Rebecca a critical look. "I told Becky we should butt out, but she's determined to talk about it."

"How did you two find out?"

Sally deferred to Rebecca who said simply, "I was driving down Motor Avenue early Christmas morning on my way to the airport when I saw you two in his car. It didn't take three years of law school to make the obvious deduction."

"We're not prying, really. It *is* your life," Sally assured Devon.

"But you think it's stupid," Devon said to Rebecca.

"Well, it's certainly a complication you don't need."

"I'm aware of that. I've been telling myself that very thing since the first minute I laid eyes on that man." Devon sighed, then looked at her two friends helplessly. "As you can see, I haven't listened to myself."

"Devon, it's obvious you're in love," Sally responded. "I, for one, am happy for you."

"Thanks, Sally," Devon said, but she continued to look at Rebecca.

"So where do you go from here?" Rebecca asked. "You know we'll keep our mouths shut, Dev. But others won't. It'll get out. It's only a question of time."

"I know. I'm amazed it's not common knowledge right now."

"I'm really not prying, Dev," Rebecca said with uncharacteristic gentleness in her voice. "I'm concerned. I just don't see how you're going to work this out. You can't marry the guy and both of you continue working at UFS."

"Oh, Rebecca, stop acting like Devon's committed some unpardonable sin," Sally said angrily. "She has the right to fall in love."

"I know what Rebecca's getting at," Devon said. She appreciated Sally's defense, but she knew Rebecca was right. "I'm in a definite conflict-of-interest situation here."

Rebecca cocked her head to one side and eyed her friend thoughtfully. "You're not thinking of going all domestic, are you? Hanging up your guns and raising babies?"

"And what if she is? There's a lot to be said for that," Sally replied.

"Hey, both of you, stop it! I feel like a tennis ball being bounced back and forth between you. You're arguing about me and I don't even know what the hell I'm going to do."

"Spence could go to another studio," Sally suggested.

"No! What kind of studio chief gets rid of the most valuable producer on the lot?" Devon's voice was firm.

"Well, then, kiddo, from what I can see, you're in a real dilemma," Rebecca said.

"Tell me about it," Devon replied drily.

Rebecca rose and said with real concern, "I'm sorry

if I sound like the Devil's advocate. Despite what Sally says, I'm not opposed to love. It's just that I can see a freight train coming at you, and I don't know how you're going to get out of the way. But if there's anything I can do to help . . ."

"I know, Becky. Thanks."

There was a long pause, then Rebecca said quietly, "I envy you, you know."

"You do?" Devon was genuinely surprised. In all the years she'd known Rebecca through the Old Girls' Network, Rebecca had never given any indication that she was looking for true love. Short, passionate affairs were much more her style. "Why do you envy me?"

"Because you love this guy enough to risk losing everything for him. I've never felt that way about anyone. I can't even imagine what that kind of love must be like. And it makes me feel that I'm missing something."

Before Devon could respond to this amazing revelation, Rebecca pulled back. "I've got to go, boss. Lots to do. Remember . . . if I can help, just let me know."

"I will. Thanks."

When Rebecca left, Sally said with studied nonchalance, "Don't pay too much attention to her, Dev. Personally I'm on your side."

"So is Rebecca. She's just being realistic."

"Well, I think she's exaggerating." Sally's hazel eyes were distracted and she nervously played with a loose button on her gray wool blazer.

As she watched her suddenly Devon realized that Sally wasn't thinking so much of her but of herself. Sally's angry reaction to Rebecca's hard but accurate words revealed a personal concern that went beyond her long-standing friendship with Devon.

"Sally, do you remember the night you and Andy Dreyfuss made love for the first time?"

Sally smiled. "I walked into the dorm, plopped down

on my bed and the first words out of your mouth were 'Get down to the med center tomorrow and start taking the pill.'"

"Sally, you were totally unprepared."

"I wasn't *planning* on what happened," Sally answered defensively.

"Of course not. You were a romantic. So was I, for that matter. But we're not giddy twenty-year-olds anymore. The stakes have grown considerably beyond a mere broken heart. I think Rebecca's words have some validity for both of us."

Sally threw Devon a startled, wary look. Then she sighed heavily and her shoulders sagged, as if she had been fighting hard and was now weary of the fight. A wistful look came over her soft, lovely features, and for a moment Devon thought how terribly young and vulnerable she seemed.

"Do you remember, Dev, how you used to tell me that God must be holding an umbrella over my head to protect me from bad things, because I was so naive yet never got hurt?"

"Yes. You were always absolutely brilliant, but you didn't have one ounce of common sense. Yet, somehow you got by without catastrophe." She smiled and shook her head. "You must have some terrific karma."

Sally stared out the window past Devon, not quite meeting her look. "We've made it, haven't we? I suppose other women envy us, especially you. But you know what? It hasn't turned out at all the way I expected."

"I know." Devon's tone was warm with understanding.

"Well, I'd better get going too," Sally said abruptly, as if just realizing she had said too much. "We're going to start shooting soon, and there's still so much to do."

"Keep me posted."

"I will."

When Sally had gone, Devon sat quietly for a while. She considered Rebecca's words. "I can see a freight train coming at you and I don't see how you're going to get out of the way."

Well, I don't know, either, Devon thought soberly. But there's *got* to be a way somehow.

Chapter 17

FILMING OF *LAST CHANCE* BEGAN ON JANUARY SECOND IN Banff, in the Canadian Rockies of Alberta Province, with Kreiss shooting only the big exteriors. In two months the company would return to Hollywood to finish the picture on local location and sound-stage sets. Anxiously Devon watched reports of the weather in the Canadian Rockies. But it held clear, with no storms and only light snowfall, coming usually at night.

Three days after shooting began, Devon and Spence went down to a screening room to view the first dailies. Devon was as excited as she had been as a child on Christmas morning, opening her gifts. The shooting schedule indicated three scenes to be shot, coming about halfway through the script, when the mother and daughter were left alone in a cabin while their men went to hunt for food.

Spence settled into one of the big sofa-chairs flanking the console that connected with the projection room behind and above them, then he hit the intercom: "We're ready anytime you are." The lights went down and the first reel began.

But as she watched the dailies, take after take of the same close-up, abortive cuts and innumerable pickups, Devon's elation began to evaporate, her confidence to waver. There was something definitely wrong. The film they were looking at had no vitality, the performances of a fine—and expensive—cast seemed labored, grudgingly produced. And it was slow to the point of being deadly dull.

When the last reel ended and the lights came up, Spence angrily stabbed the intercom. "Is that all?" he demanded.

The filtered voice of the projectionist responded, "That's all we've got up here."

Spence turned to Devon, his eyes blazing. "Correct me if I'm wrong, but it looks to me like after the first day of shooting, we're already a half day behind schedule!"

"It's only the first day," Devon countered defensively. "You know as well as I do that the first day of a shoot can be a killer. I'm sure Sally knows how to make it up."

"She'd better," he snapped. Then he shook his head. "That's not even the biggest problem. I'm not impressed with any of it: the lighting, his choice of coverage and especially the performances. I think he's going to have to reshoot the whole damned thing!"

His arbitrary tone irritated Devon, but in her heart she was afraid he might be right. Something was definitely wrong up there, and at $80,000 per day the cost of a major problem added up very quickly. She swallowed her indignation and nodded. "I'm going to get on the phone with Sally and talk to her."

"Good," Spence said. Then, realizing he'd been a bit heavy-handed, he added more reasonably, "We'll see more stuff tomorrow, Devon. Maybe we'll be pleasantly surprised."

But, Devon realized, his voice didn't carry much conviction. And her own mind was far from at ease with what she'd seen that morning.

That night Devon worked late, waiting with growing annoyance for Sally to return the call she'd placed immediately upon returning to her office from the screening room. Finally, at ten P.M., Sally called.

"Dev, I'm sorry it took so long to get back to you, but it's been real hectic. One of the stuntmen broke a leg this morning and it's jammed everything up."

"How is he?" Devon asked with real alarm.

"He'll be fine. We got him to the hospital in Banff. The stunt coordinator has arranged for a replacement to fly up from LA tomorrow."

"What happened, Sally?"

Sally hesitated, then replied rather evasively, "It was a fall . . . you know, in the avalanche scene. He didn't land right. It wasn't anybody's fault."

But Devon knew that well-directed stunts weren't supposed to go wrong. And when they did, it was usually the fault of a director who demanded too dangerous an angle.

"Sally, I don't want anyone else getting hurt up there. And I want you to tell Karl to call me tomorrow night. I want to make sure he understands that."

"Oh, he does, Dev," Sally said quickly. "I don't think there's any point in talking to him. I told you, it wasn't anybody's fault."

With growing annoyance Devon snapped, "Sally, I don't think you heard me. I said I want to talk to Karl. Now, if they don't wrap in time for him to get me at the office, tell him to call me at home."

There was a chilly silence. Then Sally finally replied, "All right. I'll tell him." But it was obvious she resented Devon's intrusion.

"I saw the dailies," Devon said. "There are some things we've got to talk about. Frankly I was disappointed." Might as well get it all on the table, Devon thought.

There was another awkward silence; Devon almost felt sorry for her friend on the other end of the line. She understood the pressure Sally was under. But they were both big girls now, each with a job to do. "I know what you saw may have seemed a little slow," Sally conceded. "But it will work beautifully in context with everything else." She added eagerly, "Wait until you see what we shot today, Dev. It's fantastic!"

"I hope you're right," Devon said. "But there's also the schedule problem."

"Not a problem," Sally countered confidently. "The first day was a madhouse. But last night I sat down with Karl and we figured out how to pick up the stuff we missed."

"Okay, put a copy of the revised schedule in the pouch tomorrow. I want to see exactly what the plan is."

The chilly edge returned to Sally's voice. "Sure. But I was hoping you'd trust me on that one. We've got to be able to play it by ear up here. It's not exactly like shooting on the back lot."

The patronizing tone ignited Devon's temper. "Sally, I think I have a pretty fair idea of the difficulties of shooting on distant location. Just make sure that the revised shooting schedule comes in with the film tomorrow night."

Realizing she might have pushed Devon too far, Sally adopted a conciliatory tone. "Sure. Good night, Dev. And don't worry. The shoot's going fine."

When Devon hung up, she sat in the silent office for a long while, thinking about her awkward conversation with Sally. She felt strongly that something was wrong on *Last Chance*, but she wanted desperately for Sally to bring the picture in. As she slipped on her coat and walked downstairs to her car she felt uneasy, and she felt uneasier yet when, driving home, she realized that were anyone but Sally on the picture, she would already be making contingency plans for a replacement.

The next day's *Last Chance* film was a slight improvement, but hardly the fantastic dailies Sally had promised. They fell into a routine: Each morning she and Spence would meet at a screening room and he would launch a running, and increasingly harsh, criticism of the film they were watching, while Devon defended, with a growing lack of conviction, Sally's ability to run the production. The situation was rapidly building to a head, and Devon knew that Spence was waiting impatiently for her to make a move.

Devon took Sally's revised shooting schedule home with her over the weekend. She discovered with angry chagrin that Kreiss's plan for making up the lost days involved extending the distant location shooting and trimming scenes from the material to be shot when the company returned to the studio. It was unconscionable that Sally had not cleared the proposal with Devon before committing it to paper. That evening she called location, reaching Terry Bernstein, the production manager.

"Terry, why didn't you call me when you got this revised schedule?"

There was a note of genuine puzzlement in Bernstein's voice when he replied, "Call you? Sally told me she'd cleared it from the top. It didn't make sense to me, but I've got a madhouse on my hands up here. . . ."

Devon swallowed her indignation. "How bad is it, Terry?"

"The worst week of my life. And I've gone through divorce and open-heart surgery. How's that for bad?

Your man Kreiss can't seem to make up his mind what he wants. He's burning film like it's confetti. And as far as alienating people—and I mean cast and crew—he's a walking original. You haven't even seen the overtime sheets yet. . . ."

Devon cut off the outburst. It was obvious Bernstein could go on for some time. "I get the picture. Thanks."

After hanging up, Devon immediately dialed again, making reservations for two on the first flight on Monday morning for Calgary.

Then she phoned Spence at home. She got straight to the point. "We've got to get up there and straighten things out."

"I agree. I was going to talk to you in the morning about the same thing."

"I'll have a car sent out to take you to the airport."

"Devon," Spence said, "I'm sorry."

She hung up, feeling a desolation and sense of frustration that threatened to overwhelm her. And beneath it all was a fierce anger with Sally's performance. Her behavior had not only jeopardized the picture but Devon's position. And she was supposed to be a friend.

The three-hour flight to Alberta the next morning was uneventful; both Devon and Spence pointedly avoided any discussion of *Last Chance;* there would be time enough for that after they met with Sally and Kreiss. Devon had purposely not telephoned Sally to tell her they were coming. The time for diplomacy, even for friendship, was past; now it was time for the hard business realities of picture-making to take over.

Spence drove the rental car the eighty or so miles from the sprawling city of Calgary to the Banff resort. Had she not been so preoccupied, Devon would have enjoyed the excursion immensely. Even so, her heart leaped at the towering, snowy crags of the Canadian

Rockies and the vast glacial valleys carved so many centuries ago when the earth was young. Neither the earth nor the phenomenal success story, Devon O'Neill, was quite so young anymore, she thought wryly. And she had a strong feeling that she would be feeling considerably older yet before the day was done.

A broad stone bridge spanned the icy Bow River between the quaint little resort town and the Banff Springs Hotel. The hotel was a towering stone castle of the European mold built a hundred or more years earlier by the Canadian Pacific Railroad to lure vacationers and generate passenger traffic for its new route westward over the Rockies. Spence pulled into the broad courtyard overlooking a frozen lake and the sweeping river plain. Devon, bundled in a white fox-fur parka, could only wish she and Spence had come to this romantic hideaway for an idyllic interlude of skiing and making love, with the trauma and heartache of picture-making left somewhere far away.

But that was not the case, and what had to be done was better done quickly. They registered, in separate rooms, ordered their bags taken up and went straight to the production offices, located in two long trailers stationed in an out-of-the-way hotel employees' parking lot. Their unexpected arrival caused the expected stir; Bernstein, the production manager, glanced up from a desk cluttered with shooting schedules, time cards and call sheets, and swallowed hard. "Surprise," he said weakly.

Surprise indeed, Devon thought. After the formalities Bernstein quickly rustled up a driver and a big four-by-four utility van, with snow-crusted chains on the tires, to take them up to location on a railroad siding some twenty miles distant.

Sally was waiting as the van pulled up; she was dressed in a faded green military parka and thermal boots, her breath smoking on the frosty air. Devon knew that Bernstein would have radioed ahead to the set, warning her of their arrival. Sally looked nervous, she thought, as well she should. But she managed a chipper smile as they stepped out of the van. "You two have got to be crazy, trading Beverly Hills sunshine for *this!*"

But once the ammenities were behind them, Spence minced no words. "We've got problems, Sally. And they've got to be handled now."

A hundred or so yards away the company was setting up a shot, but even at that distance Devon could feel that every cast and crew member was intensely aware of the meeting going on between their producer and the top studio brass.

A note of alarm crept into Sally's voice as she glanced anxiously at Devon. "You're not going to shut us down, are you?"

"That depends," Devon said. There was no sense in allowing Sally to believe the situation wasn't absolutely critical. "Whatever we do, some changes are going to have to be made."

Suddenly Sally's voice went ragged. "Well, I don't think it's fair! Karl is working his heart out! It may just be that neither of you understand what he's trying to accomplish!"

Devon could hardly believe the childish outburst, and Spence's eyes blazed with fury. "I don't know what business you think you're in, Sally, but it's not picture-making! And you'd better get yourself under control!"

Devon quickly stepped between the two of them, turning on her producer. "Sally, that was a stupid thing to say, and I'm trusting that you realize it. You tell Karl that we'll all look at rushes together this evening and then meet in my rooms afterward!"

Sally stared at Devon, her chin trembling. Then she

turned on her heel, jammed her fists into the big pockets of her parka and strode away through the snow. Beyond her Devon could see Kreiss in the middle of the set, shouting directions, flanked by a train-mounted Panaflex and two Arriflexes on tripods. A second Panaflex on a crane truck was churning through the snow into the desired position.

Devon sighed. "He's got enough equipment up here to shoot *War and Peace.*"

"And he's taking longer to film it than Tolstoy did to write it," Spence said. He turned to Devon. "You don't have a problem on your hands, Devon. You've got a disaster."

He held her eyes for a moment, and Devon knew that his use of the word *you* wasn't an accident. And he was right; it was *her* responsibility to make the fix. If a fix could be made.

Then Spence looked away, shaking his head. "Let's get back to the hotel. We're only going to be a distraction up here."

They viewed the rushes in an unoccupied banquet room of the hotel. Kreiss and Sally were late in arriving; she looking like a coiled spring about to snap, and he in an agitated mood, chain-smoking ciga-rettes and adopting an abrasive tone. Spence appeared to ignore Karl, but he muttered under his breath for Devon's benefit, "He's high as a kite." Devon didn't need to be told.

The film was no improvement over what they'd seen previously, and the gathering adjourned to Devon's rooms, where she began without preamble, "You're two and a half days behind schedule. You're way over budget, and everyone in the company is at each other's throats. And not only that, you've both lied to me. The truth is, I don't know if anything can be salvaged. You're going to have to convince me."

"Devon, you don't have any idea what conditions have been like—" Sally said, her voice nearly pleading. Spence stood at the window, watching Devon carefully.

Devon interrupted Sally, looking at Kreiss. "I'd like to hear directly from you."

"I don't think I've got anything to defend!" he said angrily. "And I resent being called up here like this. I ought to be preparing for tomorrow's work!"

"If you're not careful, Karl, there won't be a tomorrow's work!" Devon snapped, silencing the outburst. She was aware of Sally's frightened eyes on her, but there was no way Devon could ease the ordeal for her friend. "As far as I'm concerned, you've indulged yourself at the expense of the picture and the people who are working with you! I've had to deal with prima donnas before, but at least they knew how to bring in a picture. Now all this nonsense is going to cease immediately or I'm taking you off the picture as of right now!"

Her eyes were blazing as the anger that had been building inside her ever since she viewed the first morning's dailies finally found release.

Karl stared back at her, livid with rage, his fists trembling at his side.

For a moment he looked capable of violence. Spence stepped warily nearer. Then suddenly Karl seemed to realize the position he was in. He launched into a rambling monologue about the problems on *Last Chance,* blaming everyone except himself for the setbacks.

Devon glanced at Sally. But Sally, clearly realizing how pitifully thin Karl's apology sounded, couldn't meet her eyes.

It was pointless to continue, Devon decided. When the director seemed to have run down somewhat, she said quietly, "I won't keep you any longer. I don't think there's any more to be accomplished tonight."

Karl looked at her uncertainly. Then he nodded.

"Sure." He picked up his shooting script and started for the door. "Come on, Sally."

But Devon stopped her. "Sally, just a minute. I'd like to talk to you."

Sally looked wary, even terrified. For a moment Devon felt intensely uncomfortable. This was her friend, a person she cared deeply for. But the ordeal wasn't quite finished yet.

"Go ahead," Sally told Karl.

Shaking his head, Karl left the room.

Sally turned on Devon. "You're making a terrible mistake! He wasn't himself tonight. The stress of the picture, then you two showing up out of the blue . . ."

"Sally," Spence said firmly, although not unkindly, "it's too late to try to protect him. You've got to think about yourself. You've launched a promising career. But Karl is going down, and he's about to drag you with him."

Sally recoiled from Spence. "No!" she said desperately. "If you'll just give him a little time!"

"Sally, *please!*" Devon wanted urgently to make her nearly hysterical friend understand that any further defense of her lover was hopeless. "There *isn't* any more time." She sighed. "I'm sorry, but I'm going to tell Karl he's off the picture first thing in the morning. We're going to shut down production temporarily until we can decide where to start picking up the pieces."

Sally's eyes filled with tears and her mouth quivered helplessly as her fragile self-control disintegrated completely. "Please, Dev," she whispered. "Don't do this. You don't understand. I love him . . . this will ruin everything."

For one awful moment Devon felt utterly sick inside. She'd survived so much vicious infighting during her rise through the studios. She'd been fired herself once and had been forced to fire others when they proved incompetent. But this horrible, embarrassing scene affected her more deeply than any previous experience. At that moment she hated not only what had to be done but herself as well.

She searched for something to say to Sally but could find no words.

Spence gave her a concerned look, then gently took Sally's arm. "Come on, Sally, it's time we all got some rest. I'll walk you down."

They left, Sally almost numbly following Spence's lead. Devon sank into a chair. Pulling her knees up, she wrapped her arms around them and hugged herself desperately. When Spence returned five minutes later, Devon was staring fixedly into the fire. One tear had escaped her tormented blue eyes and slithered down her cheek.

Spence reached out with one finger and gently wiped the tear away. He began gently, "She understands she'll have to go too." Then, when Devon said nothing, he added, "It had to be done, Devon. He ruined this picture and she let him do it. I know she's your friend, but . . ."

"It isn't just that," Devon interrupted, looking up at him helplessly. "I understand why she did it. How it happened. She's a good producer, but . . . she made the mistake of trying to have her career and the man she loved too. Oh, God, when I think what I'm doing to her . . ."

"Devon, she did it to herself," Spence snapped. But he added with more compassion, "Nobody ever said it was going to be easy."

Devon forced herself to smile, but there was little conviction in it. Spence nodded, "That's better. Now I'll start taking care of the nuts and bolts. You get some sleep. I know what an ordeal that was for you, and tomorrow morning isn't going to be a piece of cake either."

Spence picked up the phone and dialed Terry Bernstein's room, ordering the production manager to cancel all the next morning's shooting calls and assemble the production staff immediately for an emergency meeting in his rooms. Devon admired the clipped efficiency and easy authority with which he set about shutting down a multimillion-dollar motion picture production as though he were ordering food to go from a restaurant. Perhaps Spence had been right that very first day; perhaps the game *was* too tough for a woman. She wondered if she would ever regain the unqualified confidence in her decision-making ability that had carried her so far. At the moment she was far from sure.

Spence hung up the phone, lifted her to her feet and gave her a tender kiss. "Try to put it out of your mind. It may feel like the end of the world right now, but it's not. And you handled an awful scene with a lot of class. If anything, Devon, I admire you more."

She forced another smile for his benefit. But she still felt sick at heart. And she knew it would be a long time before that sick feeling went away.

Her expected confrontation with Karl Kreiss the following morning never materialized. Devon was awakened by a phone call from a weary Terry Bernstein, who, with Spence and most of his production supervisors, had been up most of the night.

"Dev," Bernstein said, "Spence asked me to tell you that Karl's gone. Sally too. They left last night. I expect his lawyers will be in touch."

Devon sighed. She hadn't been looking forward to firing Kreiss formally, but she had wanted some time alone with Sally, since their meeting had ended on such an ugly note. But that was not to be, and she forced herself to address the matters at hand.

"Thank you, Terry," she said. "What's our situation?"

"Grim, but Spence wants to fill you in on it himself.

We're all to meet in your rooms at eleven, if that's okay with you."

"Fine, I'll see you then."

Grim. She hadn't expected the morning to bring anything *but* grim news, she mused as she gazed out the frosty window of her sitting room. Long daggers of icicles, gleaming in the morning sunshine, hung like fangs from the eaves of the roof. Far below she could see two down-jacket clad young lovers having a snowball fight on the hotel's broad sweep of lawn, the girl laughing and shaking loose snow out of her long, auburn hair. For a moment Devon suffered an irrational stab of panic, afraid that she would never again be able to take pleasure in so simple a frolic as the girl below was enjoying with her young man, afraid that she was a fool—or worse, a foolish *woman*—for striving so hard and reaching so high. For an instant she was filled with an overwhelming impulse to flee, to run as fast and as far away from this place as she could.

But the moment passed. She smiled wryly; the problem with running away, as the man said, was that you couldn't leave yourself behind, and wherever you went, that simple fact spoiled everything. She pulled herself up with new determination. Besides, she thought, *Last Chance* is a sound project. It's worth saving. And that's exactly what I intend to do.

But it wouldn't be easy. That fact became painfully clear at the eleven o'clock meeting, when Spence arrived with Terry Bernstein and his assistants and the adding machines began to spit out the reality of their situation. *Last Chance* was a sick patient indeed.

Two hours later Bernstein leaned back in his chair with a helpless gesture. "There it is," he said. "The picture's a week behind schedule and three quarters of a million over. Kreiss had a play-or-pay deal, so we're in for his full three-hundred-fifty thousand. If we start up again, we've got to extend the shooting schedule, and that means we lose our lady lead. We have to pay her off and recast. Another million five and change. And that's *if* we can find another director on a week's notice." He shook his head. "Bottom line, Devon: three million dollars' worth of red ink. I'm sorry."

Devon thanked Bernstein, and he read it accurately as an invitation to leave. She and Spence alone would determine the fate of *Last Chance*.

When the production people were gone, Devon turned passionately to Spence. "This picture can be salvaged! I know it can, Spence!" Her fighting spirit had returned, as it usually did when the odds against her mounted. She still felt badly for Sally, but her main concern now was saving the picture.

Spence shook his head impatiently. "You're talking about throwing good money after bad. By the time this thing's finished, *if* there aren't any more snafus, it's going to cost so much it will be nearly impossible to recoup our losses."

"Unless it goes through the ceiling," Devon countered. "And I happen to believe it will."

He turned to face her squarely, and a new note of gravity crept into his voice, one that triggered a stab of alarm in Devon even before she'd heard him out.

"I'm not prepared to gamble that it will, Devon. My company can't sustain a loss as big as the one I see coming here. I'm sorry, but I'm backing out."

Stunned, Devon finally asked, "What did you say?"

"The picture's gone more than ten percent over budget. I expect it's going to go higher than that if you try to complete it. I can't go with you, Devon. It's that simple."

Devon stared at him, her mind racing. Without Spence's support she would either have to declare the project a dead loss or commit the studio to going ahead on its own, shouldering the entire financial risk. Devon knew her job wouldn't survive the major setback of scuttling the project. But she also knew that if she committed the studio to finishing the picture and *Last Chance* failed at the box office, the loss would be even greater. In either case her job would be lost.

"Do you realize what you're saying?" she finally asked in a whisper.

Spence's green eyes were pained. When he spoke, there was a tightness in his voice that betrayed the deep conflict he felt. "Devon, I control my company. I own well over seventy percent of the shares. But I do have stockholders, some of them among my own family. It's their risk as well as mine, and I have an obligation to them. I can't knowingly send my company into bankruptcy. If I go ahead with this picture, and you're wrong and it fails, that's exactly what will happen. And I can't let my feelings for you intervene."

So it's finally happened, Devon thought numbly. Combining sex and business is a time bomb, Rebecca had said. How right she was.

"Look," Spence said angrily, "I'm not exaggerating the financial condition of my company. But it's more than that! Devon, it's a question of judgment. I don't believe it's going to work. Not now. The numbers are way out of line." He turned away, shaking his head in frustration. "I'm sorry. But we agreed to the rules going in."

They'd agreed, true, but Devon realized that, until this moment, she'd never believed he would withdraw his support. Not the man she loved. . . .

He turned back to her, his eyes imploring. "If we shut it down this afternoon, we can get out for a shade over six million. And if you'll agree to that, Devon, I'll stay on the hook for my half. I'm not contractually bound to do so, but I do share the responsibility for the failure. . . ."

Suddenly Devon was on her feet, her eyes blazing with fury. "No! You're not salving your conscience for thirty pieces of silver, Spence!" She planted herself squarely in front of him, hands on her hips. "And you're wrong! *Last Chance* was solid when we started and it's still viable. I'm moving ahead with it, whether you're part of the package or not!"

She held his angry eyes locked a moment longer, then turned away. "I'd appreciate it if you'd leave now. I've got work to do."

Spence hesitated. Obviously there was a great deal more he wanted to say. Devon looked back at him, shooting him a defiant look. "Oh, hell!" he swore explosively, and strode from the room, slamming the door after him.

Devon ordered Terry Bernstein to put the entire production of *Last Chance* on hold until further notice. That afternoon she was chauffeured to the airport at Calgary in a company car. She spent the drive furiously poring over the production staff's figures on the picture's likely deficit and assigning priorities to problems. The chief ones were recruiting a frontline director and a new female lead—chief, that is, if she could convince Harrison not to fire her on the spot when he learned what a debacle her first major outing had turned into.

It wasn't until she was on the plane, winging south over the night-shrouded Rocky Mountains below, that she allowed her thoughts to return to Spence, who had caught an earlier flight.

Her business sense said he was right: They *had* agreed to the rules going in. But the woman in her was deeply hurt and disappointed. This was the man who had lain in her arms, who had loved her as no man had done before or was likely to do again. The man in whose arms she felt safe and infinitely protected. . . .

And this was how all that love, all that physical and emotional intimacy, had ended. A casualty of egotism, ambition, harsh financial realities and God knew what else.

She would try to salvage the movie, try to save her career, because it was crucial to her sense of integrity. But all the while she was doing that, she knew she would be thinking of Spence.

After a moment she turned off the overhead light and turned her face toward the window. She didn't want anyone to see Devon O'Neill, motion picture industry wunderkind, crying softly into her airline pillow.

Chapter 18

DEVON HAD ARRANGED FOR REBECCA TO MEET HER AT LOS Angeles International Airport. She needed her friend's warmth and shrewd counsel. Rebecca was there when Devon stepped off the plane, hurrying across the crowded passenger concourse. But from her stricken expression Devon knew that something was terribly wrong.

"Devon," Rebecca said, embracing her. "Thank God you're here!"

"What is it, Becky?"

"I almost don't know how to tell you, after everything you've been through the last couple of days. But . . . it's Sally. She's in intensive care at St. John's." Rebecca took a deep breath. "Dev, she tried to kill herself."

For a stunned moment Devon's mind refused to register the information. Devon knew that Sally had taken the events in Banff hard, but *this*. . . . And it was Devon's fault: She was the one who had fired Sally. For a moment Devon thought she would collapse under the weight of the awful realization.

Rebecca gave her a concerned look and said gently, "Devon, I know you're blaming yourself and you mustn't. You gave Sally every opportunity. She let *you* down."

"No," Devon said, barely able to find her voice. "I was so concerned with the picture! I should have known—!"

"Stop it!" Rebecca snapped angrily. "You had to be concerned with the picture! And if Sally had been a little more concerned with it—and less worried about holding together a nice warm cocoon for that spoiled, arrogant louse of a boyfriend—none of this would have happened!"

On one level Devon realized her friend was right. But it had been an exhausting and emotionally trying two days, and her mind was weary, hard pressed not to seize the obvious interpretation. She glanced up at Rebecca. "How did she do it?"

"An overdose of barbiturates. Luckily, at the very last, she had a change of heart. She phoned me at the studio and I got an ambulance there just in time."

Devon frowned. "She phoned *you?* Where was Karl?"

"I wondered the same thing," Rebecca said, her tone hardening. "So I did some checking around. It seems the trials of wrecking a twenty-million-dollar motion picture exhausted him to the point that he needed a vacation. He caught a plane to the Caribbean this afternoon. Alone."

Devon stared at her. "He didn't take Sally?"

"Devon, I don't know for sure, because I haven't been able to talk to Sally, but it smells to me like he dumped her."

Devon shouldered her flight bag, her heart aching for

Sally's misery. "Becky, let's go straight to the hospital. I want to talk to her."

"You go ahead," Rebecca said grimly. "I'm going back to the studio and review Karl Kreiss's play-or-pay deal. If there's any way we can set him on the sidewalk without a nickel, I intend to find it."

Devon nodded. "Good. I'll back you to the limit. If nothing else, we can keep him in court for a couple of years before he collects. And besides, I need that three hundred and fifty thousand. We're moving ahead with *Last Chance* on our own."

Rebecca flashed her a bright smile. "Marvelous, Dev. That's my girl!"

"*If* I can get Harrison Kahn's approval."

"Mmm," Rebecca said, sobering. "I don't envy you that little chat." Then she nodded confidently. "But my money's on you, kid!"

They parted in front of the terminal, Devon bolstered by her friend's encouragement. A moment later she caught a cab and ordered the driver to take her to Santa Monica Hospital to see Sally.

It was almost midnight by the time Devon reached the hospital. The nursing supervisor informed her that Sally had regained consciousness and grudgingly allowed Devon five minutes at Sally's bedside.

Sally looked awful; her hair was damp and stringy, her lovely skin pale and dehydrated and her tormented eyes like burnt sockets. But she was alive.

Devon, hiding her alarm at Sally's devastated appearance, managed a smile. "Hi."

Sally's eyes focused on her for a moment, then filled with tears. "Oh, Dev, I'm sorry. I'm so sorry about everything!"

"Don't say a thing. Not tonight, Sally," Devon said, squeezing her hand gently. "I just wanted you to know I'm here, if there's anything in the world you need."

"You don't know how much that means to me," Sally said. "I have no right to expect it."

Devon swallowed back a pang of emotion. Sally was clearly exonerating her of any responsibility for the suicide attempt. But Devon knew she would never exonerate herself.

"Sally, we're friends. Nothing can change that."

A kaleidoscope of scenes flashed across her memory; she and Sally had gone through so many things together: the delight and disappointment of falling in love, marriage, divorce, career battles won and lost. They'd gone from being giddy college freshmen, convinced they had the world on a string, to mature women who knew that happy endings occurred much more often onscreen than off.

There was a bond between them, Devon knew, that would never be broken, no matter how terribly their friendship was tested.

Devon smiled at Sally with deep affection. "Hey, you're gonna be okay, you know. I'll come by every day."

Sally's eyes searched Devon's. "Does Karl know?" she whispered.

Devon frowned. But she couldn't tell Sally the truth—not yet. "I . . . I don't know."

Mustering another smile, she released Sally's hand. "You need to rest. I'll drop in again tomorrow."

Devon slumped wearily in the backseat of the cab that whisked her away from the hospital toward her home and a long-overdue night's sleep. She tried not to think about the corollary between Sally's experience and her own, but it was impossible not to. As the cab moved down nearly deserted streets damp with mist, she faced the awful fact that Sally's experience only underscored the impossibility of Devon and Spence's relationship. There was no way on earth they could

make it work as things stood now. All the love in the
world couldn't overcome the harsh realities they faced.

Soon, she knew, she would have to fly to New York
to try to persuade Harrison not to kill the picture—and
not to fire her.

She sighed deeply as the glistening streets slipped by
outside the windows of the cab. It seemed her life had
turned into an endless series of airplane trips and
torturous confrontations, none of which provided solu-
tions but merely bred more of the same. She felt
disoriented and utterly alone; for a moment she was
tempted to stop the cab at the nearest pay phone and
call Spence, agree to his terms for shutting down the
picture and then rush to him and the shelter of his
strong arms.

But it was only an impulse. Devon had thrown the
gauntlet down in front of him, and she knew her pride
and her professional dignity would never permit her to
pick it up again.

And that determination, she thought with a wry,
exhausted smile, would be all she'd have to keep her
warm when she reached home and slipped into her
empty bed.

Spence, also having returned from Canada the previous day, arrived at the studio in a foul mood. He strode
angrily past the elevators to the stairwell and ascended
the steps two at a time. Every muscle in his body was
tensed, as if to fight, but there was no opponent. At
least no tangible one.

"Damn!" he muttered out loud, ignoring the secretaries and production assistants he passed in the corri-
dor and drawing surprised glances.

I have nothing to feel guilty about, he told himself.
She wanted to be head of the studio; now she's got to
accept the problems that come with the territory. She
can't put the blame on me. Women! She gave her friend

a job she couldn't handle, and now she wants me to hold her hand. It was her mistake!

He pulled up, uncomfortably aware that men often did exactly the same thing; he himself had more than once let friendship tilt the balance when two reasonably equal candidates were vying for the same job. He was also well aware that Devon hadn't really hired Sally out of friendship, but at this point his anger was too great to be swayed by reason.

Anyway, he thought sourly, I told her a woman couldn't handle that job, but she wouldn't listen. Now I'm supposed to go down with the ship? Not likely!

Such were his thoughts as he slammed into his office, propelled by a towering rage. He snapped at his secretary when she made the mistake of inquiring about his trip, and his mood wasn't improved when he discovered that the headlines of the morning trade papers, waiting for him on his desk, bannered news of Kreiss's firing, with the stories quoting the director's version of events. Both he and Devon came out sounding like heavy-handed villains, ignorant of the "art of the cinema." He might have known Kreiss's first move would be to phone the trades. Spence knew he should have anticipated that and beat Kreiss to the punch.

For a moment he felt a pang of sympathy. He knew Devon would be reading the same trades and would certainly be hurt by the one-sided condemnation of their actions. He was tempted to call her and offer a word of condolence. But then he firmly put the notion aside. Bad press was an occupational hazard; it came with the territory too.

But Devon's terrible plight nagged at him the rest of the day as he drafted a scathing rebuttal to Kreiss's version of events and disposed of a hundred other lesser problems routine to his working day. Try as he might not to face the truth, he was deeply worried about how she was holding up.

Devon's own day unfolded much as she had expected, beginning with a phone call to Harrison Kahn, reassuring him that the situation on *Last Chance* was in hand and informing him that she would fly east on Friday to brief him in detail.

"Are you going to pull the plug?" he asked, his tone betraying no feelings he might have one way or the other.

"My inclination is no," Devon said carefully. "Subject to your approval, of course."

"I see," he said mildly. "Well, I'll look forward to a very interesting meeting on Friday."

Devon was buoyed by the conversation; she'd opened the door on the possibility of saving her picture, and it hadn't been slammed in her face. She was further encouraged when a jubilant Rebecca sailed into her office with news that Karl Kreiss's contract might not be as ironclad as they'd feared.

"I'm going to use the performance clause in his contract to whipsaw the little rodent out of his back teeth," she gloated.

"He can keep his teeth," Devon laughed. "All we want is our money."

Rebecca shot her a look. "Obviously you haven't read the trades, or you wouldn't be feeling quite so agreeable."

Devon frowned and picked up *Variety*, quickly scanning the Kreiss version of the Banff fiasco. She didn't bother with *The Hollywood Reporter;* she knew it would carry substantially the same story. Raw anger welled up within her, but also an involuntary stab of pain that Spence, whose taste and integrity were legendary in the business, should find himself sharing the brunt of such an attack from such an insignificant source. For a moment she was tempted to pick up the telephone and tell him exactly that, but she forced herself to reject the impulse. He might very well interpret it as a sign of weakness.

She tossed the newspaper aside and nodded grimly to Rebecca. "You're absolutely right, counselor. Go for his teeth."

The rest of the day was devoted to determining the availability of frontline directors and ranking leading women, and by the end of it Devon realized she had a big problem on her hands. The directors whose style and technique she believed fit the project were locked up on other pictures, and the same held true for the female stars she favored.

"It always boils down to who's available," she sighed as Rebecca joined her for a cup of tea at the end of the day. "And this time nobody is."

"I may have an idea," Rebecca said thoughtfully. "It would be a gamble, but you're in no position to do anything else, and it would fill the director's slot anyway."

"Who?" Devon asked eagerly.

Rebecca reminded her of a young director-editor team, husband and wife, who had just broken out of television with a low-budget horror film that was widely hailed for its innovative technique and classic style and concept. And for doing superb box office.

"Sean Randall is the director," Rebecca said. "His wife is Nora. I met them at a party in Benedict Canyon the other night. I liked them both. They might be worth considering."

Devon knew the film; in fact, she had made a mental note to investigate the people behind it. But that had been before Banff.

"I think it's a brilliant idea, Becky." She picked up the phone, asking her secretary to contact the Randalls' agent and set up a meeting for the following morning if the pair was available. It turned out that they were.

"Well, I feel a little better. Let's just hope we can make it work." She glanced at her watch. "I've got to run. I promised Sally I'd drop in sometime today."

Rebecca frowned. "I saw her at lunch. The whole Karl thing has really taken the wind out of her. I didn't tell her we were going after his contract. I honestly didn't know how she'd take it."

Rebecca hadn't exaggerated. An hour later Devon found Sally looking little improved from the previous night, although she was out of intensive care and lodged in a bright, airy room on a lower floor. Devon tried to brighten her spirits.

"Now look, Sally, I know you went through hell, and there's probably more in store. But life goes on and it's time we looked ahead to your getting out of here and putting your career back on track."

Sally glanced at her, "What do you mean?"

"You're coming back to UFS—that's what I mean. Not on *Last Chance,* of course. But in your old job as a production vice-president."

Sally stared at her, then shook her head. "Dev, I don't know if I can handle it. Everything looks so black. . . ."

"I know," Devon said sympathetically. "But you're going to find help, and after a while it won't seem so black. And I intend to keep you too busy to brood. . . ."

But Sally turned anguished eyes on her. "Dev, he didn't even call. . . ." she whispered.

Devon stared at her. Still Karl Kreiss, she thought, and suddenly all her anger and frustration erupted. "Of course he didn't call, Sally! Selfish, frightened little *users* like Karl Kreiss never call! I know: I was married to one and I can give you chapter and verse!"

Sally looked up at her, startled. But Devon had only

begun. "Listen to me, Sally; Karl is ancient history now if you'll make him that. But if you don't he—or the next one like him—is going to destroy you! And if that happens, there's going to be no one to blame but yourself!"

Devon could have said more, but she already regretted having come down so hard on her friend; it was obvious Sally was near tears.

Abruptly she turned to go but stopped at the door. "The job is there if you want it, Sally," she said gently, and added, "You're a bright talent; please don't throw yourself away."

Devon drove home feeling miserable, reviewing in her mind the scene with Sally. She knew that what she'd said to her friend had to be said. But perhaps it had been too soon . . . perhaps it should have come from a psychiatrist or at least someone who hadn't been so deeply involved in the events that had led to Sally's attempted suicide. Dismally she concluded there was no way of knowing; what was done was done.

The phone was ringing as she let herself into the house. It was her mother, who, in Palm Springs, had belatedly heard of the devastating articles in the trade papers.

"It's your first bad review, darling," Sheila said sympathetically. "Just try to keep your chin up. Take it from a veteran; you'll get in your licks."

Cheered, Devon smiled. "Oh, Mother, you never had a bad review in your life."

"None that I ever let you see," Sheila laughed. "And by the time you were old enough to read them for yourself, I had wisely retired."

Devon chatted with her mother a few moments longer and then hung up and readied herself for bed and another long day.

As she slipped between the beige satin sheets, thoroughly exhausted, her mind ranged back over the events of the day, lingering on that moment when she'd been tempted to pick up the telephone and call Spence to reassure him that he was the best the game of motion picture–making had to offer. The *very* best, she thought fervently, and in so many different ways. Simply to have heard his voice . . . She hugged a fluffy pillow fiercely, but it did nothing to relieve the longing that she felt in the depths of her very soul. Finally she drifted into a troubled sleep.

Spence lay alone in his bed, watching the shifting patterns the moonlight cast on the darkened walls. The sound of the Malibu surf was low, muted yet inexorable. As inexorable as the thought of Devon that kept intruding, unbidden, into his mind.

I'm right, he told himself for the thousandth time that day. But he was also alone, bereft of Devon's warm, pliant body next to his.

"She's crazy to go ahead with this," he said out loud to no one but himself.

But deep inside he knew that all the self-righteousness in the world wouldn't disguise the loss he felt. In a brief two months she had become part of the fabric of his life. What she gave him couldn't be measured, couldn't even be put into words. He only knew that, without her, nothing else mattered.

It was nearly dawn before he fell asleep in his lonely bed. And when he awoke, he automatically reached for her.

But she wasn't there.

The single stroke of genius that made Devon's desperate attempt to resuscitate *Last Chance* a practical possibility came to her as she was driving to work the following morning, musing about her conversation with her mother the night before. It might work! she thought, smacking the steering wheel. And the more she thought about it, the more convinced she was that it *would* work. Now, she prayed desperately, if only the Randalls—the director husband—editor wife team— would work out. She strode into her office in a jubilant mood.

Sean Randall and his wife, Nora, were waiting for her in the outer office. He proved to be a burly, wool-shirted young giant with a ruddy complexion, a flaming red beard and an amused twinkle in his eye, who seemed to occupy almost all of the space in whatever room he happened to find himself. Devon liked him at first glance and liked him more when he swallowed her small hand in both his great paws and greeted her by saying, "Miss O'Neill, you wouldn't have asked me up here if you weren't in trouble on *Last Chance,* and I promise I wouldn't be here if I didn't think I could save your picture. So why don't we dispense with the usual cow chips and get down to business."

Nora, Randall's wife, a dark-complexioned wisp of a thing with feisty brown eyes, who Devon could see at a glance adored her brawny, bellicose husband, laughed unselfconsciously. "Sean's problem has always been a terrible lack of self-confidence, Miss O'Neill."

Instantly convinced that she'd found her director, Devon joined in the laughter, and in moments they were all on first-name terms. It turned out that Randall had read the script of *Last Chance* when it was being circulated among the agencies during preproduction and was excited about it.

After a few minutes of small talk they adjourned to a screening room where Devon had arranged for selected reels of Kreiss's Banff dailies to be shown. Sean Randall watched the film, muttering to himself with growing irritation and finally rising to his feet in disgust. "That's enough for me. I don't want to see any more.

Whatever Karl Kreiss's problem is, it might be catching."

Devon smiled. "Am I to understand you would take a different approach?"

"I'd put some life in the damned thing, have some fun with it, if that's what you're talking about!" he roared with disarming relish. "Hell yes, I'd take a different approach! I've been to funerals that had more vitality than what you've got in the can right now, Devon!"

"Darling, lower the volume a bit," Nora chided him affectionately. "You're not on the floor of the Grand Canyon."

Devon laughed. "Let him roar, Nora. I happen to agree with him one hundred percent."

But back in her office she adopted a serious tone. "Sean, there are two problems. One, we must resume shooting on Monday in Banff. Can you do it?"

He nodded, eyes narrowing. "I can do it. I don't know how, but I can do it."

"We're going to be on a tight schedule," she warned. "Very tight."

Sean laughed. "If you're asking me if can I gun and run, you're looking at the master. Television taught me that if nothing else."

"The second problem is the tough one," Devon said. "We're three million over. I can't offer you a lot of money up front—"

Sean leaned forward, his eyes dancing. "You *could* offer me a three-picture deal, the terms to be negotiated after *Last Chance* opens. If it's a hit, I'll recoup down the line. If not"—he shrugged with a laugh— "what the hell, we'll all be looking for work anyway."

Devon smiled, totally charmed by the man's total confidence in his ability. She offered him her hand, "In that case I think you'd better get to work."

* * *

Spence threw himself into his work that day, skipping lunch and pushing himself—and his staff—even harder than usual. When his secretary left that evening, muttering something under her breath about not being a beast of burden, he continued on, poring over budget analyses for new projects, jotting terse memos to be transcribed the next day. It was nearly midnight when he finally stopped. He threw down the pen on his desk, rubbing his eyes tiredly. It was time to quit, he knew, before he fell asleep at his desk.

His parking space was in the lot behind the executive office building. As he walked to his car, keys in hand, he glanced up. There was one light on in the building. He realized with a start that it was Devon's office. She was still there.

He hesitated, his keys in his hand. His stubborn pride and his love for Devon warred within him.

Love won.

Chapter 19

DEVON SAT AT HER DESK, GOING OVER THE FIGURES FOR the dozenth time. She'd long since kicked off the fleece-lined boots she'd worn that morning. Under the desk she rubbed her feet together numbly, but still she worked on. She would need every fact at her instant command when she sat down with Harrison Kahn in New York on Friday. But now her earlier despair had turned to elation. She was convinced—particularly with Sean Randall committed—beyond any question of doubt that she could salvage *Last Chance*.

But despite all of that, Spence continued to trouble her. She'd tried to relegate him to the back of her mind, but it hadn't worked. All day long, every time her secretary buzzed her, she'd expected to hear that he was waiting to see her. But he hadn't called. And he hadn't come. And she was alone.

And she'd managed to let him intrude into her thoughts once more, interrupting her concentration.

"Oh, hell!" she said aloud, pushing the stack of papers aside in frustration.

It was then that she heard a step outside. She frowned; it couldn't be the cleaning crew, she knew, because they'd already come. She looked up, wondering if it was the night watchman. The door opened slowly.

It was Spence.

Neither of them spoke. For a long moment they simply looked at each other, the way a man dying of thirst in the desert looks at a mirage of water.

Devon thought she'd never been so happy to see anyone in her life. The dull ache that had filled her breast for a day and a night was stilled.

He came, she thought. I don't even care what he says. All that matters is that he came.

He walked across the room to her, around the desk to where she sat. He pulled her up into his arms. There was a profoundly concerned look in his eyes. He started to speak, but Devon pressed her fingertips against his lips to stop him.

"No. Let's not talk now."

He understood. His eyes were lit by desire as he led her to the long, wide sofa. Then he pulled her against him and his mouth molded to hers in a kiss so possessive that it left Devon weak and shaken. The hunger in his kiss ran through her, igniting her like a match set to tinder-dry wood.

Until that moment she hadn't realized how profoundly the thought of never being with him again had affected her. His touch was electric. Her body responded as his hands slid around her back, stroking her softly before stopping at the base of her spine.

Molded to him, she felt his desire and knew that he needed her as desperately as she needed him.

He buried his face in her silken hair and whispered

her name over and over, as if it were a magic incantation.

"Devon, my Devon . . ."

She wrapped her arms tightly around his neck, threading her fingers through his golden hair.

His fingertips kneaded the firm contours of her derriere. Then one hand moved up to push back the tousled hair from her face as he took her parted lips in a briefer, harder kiss.

She inhaled his heady scent as he rained kisses along her throat and her heart pounded erratically. Her breasts rose and fell rapidly under the cashmere sweater and wool challis skirt she'd worn that day.

Watching her, his green eyes darkened with desire. Her arms clung to the nape of his neck. Her own eyes widened with expectation. While one hand cupped her cheek, the other slid across her back to her rib cage, then moved up under the sweater to cup her breast. She was naked under the silk knit camisole she wore. In response to his searing touch, her breast trembled. As his thumb circled the nipple slowly, seductively, it hardened.

Her blood surged restlessly and she wanted nothing more than to be part of him, *there, then*.

His hands moved down to her shoulders to embrace her trembling body. His lips explored the wildly beating pulse at the base of her slender throat.

Deftly, in one swift movement, he pulled off her sweater and skirt. Now she wore only the peach-colored camisole and matching bikini panties.

At the bodice of the camisole was a see-through lace butterfly that reached nearly to the tips of her breasts. Spence's eyes seemed to devour her as he murmured, "God, you're beautiful!"

He kissed her bare shoulders, her throat, the hollow between her breasts, stopping only at the lacy butterfly.

Then he slipped the narrow straps from her shoulders and pulled the camisole below her breasts. He quickly took the erect pink tip of one breast into his mouth, his teeth teasing it gently. The moist warmth of his tongue flicking back and forth rocked her to her very center, sending a thrill of excitement up her spine.

Her legs buckled beneath her and he held her tightly against him. Holding her pliant body, he lowered her to the sofa, letting her head rest on a wool afghan folded there. The navy-blue corduroy of the upholstery was warm and soft against her bare skin.

The relentless pounding of her heart seemed to fill the silent room.

On the sofa she pressed her limbs to his hard length. She felt her stomach clench spasmodically at his touch as his fingertips tugged at her thin silk panties. Then she was completely naked beneath him, feeling the roughness of his jeans on her smooth legs, the softness of his velour pullover against her bare breasts.

One hand cupped the back of her head while the other caressed the length of her quivering body. As he looked down at her, his green eyes smoldering with barely contained desire, her soft pink lips parted unconsciously.

A low moan that seemed torn from his throat escaped him before he kissed her again, his tongue plundering her mouth. His free hand moved up to cup her breast, and she felt him shudder with a need so deep that it almost frightened her. The hunger in his kiss was reflected in each heaving breath of his powerful chest.

Completely aroused, she arched her body beneath him, begging him to take her completely. The fabric of his clothes seemed deliciously erotic against her satiny skin. Reluctantly pulling away from his kiss, she buried her face in the softness of his shirt.

He buried his lips in her hair, murmuring words

of love and desire. "My sweetest girl . . . my darling . . ."

Then she raised her head to face him. His eyes swept over her, from the strands of hair lying across her cheek; downward over her smooth, creamy shoulders; past her tautened breasts, slender waist, the round curves of her hips and silken thighs.

The light of love in his eyes warmed her like a roaring fire on a cold night. The feel of her swollen breasts against his hard, broad chest was almost unbearable.

Her eyes must have revealed the full depth of her desire, for he moved suddenly. In a matter of seconds he, too, was naked. Their bodies joined. Instantly she was at the full peak of arousal.

The frustration and anxiety of their time apart, of the overwhelming problems that still faced them, were thrown aside as he claimed her. She welcomed him completely, sliding her arms across his back and molding herself to him.

He held her face in his hands as he looked down at her. Her heartbeat joined with his, her hips moved in unison with his. The tight feeling in the pit of her stomach increased. She felt as if someone had tied a silken ribbon around her and was pulling it tighter and tighter.

A warmth began to build within her, mounting to an inferno, spreading through her body like wildfire. She arched her neck back and Spence buried his face in the softness of her breasts as both he and Devon were consumed by the white-hot blaze. . . .

They had pulled the afghan over them and lay together in each other's arms on the sofa. Devon felt warm and safe and happy. She felt as if she could lie there forever, neither of them uttering a word, luxuriating in the intimate silence.

But there were things that had to be said.

"Do you still feel you must go through with this?"
Spence asked quietly.

She nodded.

"I'll help you, then."

She frowned, looking up at him, as she realized the
enormity of the offer he'd just made. He was willing to
risk his whole company, everything he'd worked for his
whole life, not because he believed in the project, but
because he loved her. She felt tears moisten her eyes.

"No," she finally said so softly he barely heard her.

"Devon," he said tenderly. "Don't be stubborn.
That's all behind us now."

"I'm not being stubborn," she said, smiling. "And I
know how generous your offer was. I'll never forget it.
But it wouldn't be good for us if I took you up on it."

"I don't understand."

"Your heart isn't in *Last Chance* anymore, Spence.
You'd only be doing it for me, not because you believed
in the picture. That isn't what love should be—a power
struggle, one of us trying to get the other to do
something we feel is wrong."

"Most women would enjoy the sense of victory,"
Spence commented with an amused smile.

"Don't you see," Devon said seriously, rubbing her
cheek gently against his shoulder, "I wouldn't want you
to wield that kind of power over me. So I can't do it to
you. I've got to handle this myself."

"You're absolutely sure . . . ?"

"No," she said with a low laugh. "I'm not sure of
anything. Except that if you went ahead with this
picture because of me and it failed, and because of that
your company went under . . ." She paused, shaking
her head helplessly. "I couldn't live with that."

He held her warmly and in silence for a long moment, his fingers gently massaging the nape of her neck.
Devon felt that they were as close and loving as they

could possibly be, and she was filled with a limitless contentment.

"What are you going to do?" he asked softly.

"I've made some moves. I think they're good ones. I'm going to hire Sean Randall to replace Karl . . . if I can get Harrison to give me a go-ahead to resume shooting."

There was another moment of silence, then Spence raised himself up on one arm and looked down at her soberly. "Forget Harrison. Forget the studio. Marry me, Devon." His voice had grown almost grim. Realizing that, he added self-consciously, "I love you more than I ever dreamed of loving anyone."

Devon smiled. "I know. When you offered to step back into the picture, you proved how much you loved me. I love you that much and more, darling."

She hesitated. She was strongly tempted to accept his offer. But she knew that would be running away. She would always feel that she hadn't been able to handle the pressures of power and had taken a woman's easy way out. For her own self-esteem, she realized dismally, she had to see this through.

"I can't," she said simply, and they were the hardest words she'd ever had to speak. The moment they were out, she regretted them, wished she could take them back. But she couldn't.

"Why?" he asked, not angrily but with a puzzled tenderness.

"Spence, I honestly believe *Last Chance* can be a great picture. I'm not pressing ahead out of stubbornness or pride. Don't you understand? I have to prove to myself and everyone else that I can do this job. What kind of a wife would I be to you if I despised myself?"

"But we love each other, Devon. In a way that most people only fantasize about. We both know how rare it is, how lucky we were to find each other when we'd both almost stopped hoping to find this kind of happiness."

"Sometimes all the love in the world isn't enough, Spence." She was filled with an infinite sadness. "This isn't a movie, where the hero and heroine ride off together into the sunset and live happily ever after. We have to live in the real world. I don't think our love can survive the conflicts in what we do every day behind these walls. It would be different if we worked in different fields. But I'm the president of this studio, and you're the most important producer in the USF fold. We simply can't handle the conflicts that are bound to arise from that situation. Eventually one of us would compromise the other's principles, just as yours were almost compromised tonight. And our love would never survive that."

She could see he knew she was right.

"What do you want?" he asked.

"I want to make this picture. I *have* to make this picture. But right now, tonight, I just want you to hold me one last time."

His arms enveloped her in a fierce, desperate embrace that was bittersweet in its poignancy.

Chapter 20

DEVON STEPPED OFF THE TWA RED-EYE AT KENNEDY ON Friday morning, feeling rumpled and exhausted from her fitful sleep on the plane. Nevertheless she was looking forward to the luncheon meeting with Harrison Kahn. She didn't know if he would buy her plan to salvage *Last Chance*—and if he didn't, he'd probably fire her—but she knew he'd have to listen. A limousine was waiting to carry her to the Pierre, where she'd reserved a suite to freshen up before meeting Kahn.

As she luxuriated in a hot, scented bath at the hotel her mind drifted inevitably to Spence. The overwhelming sadness she'd managed to hold at bay since their tryst in her office welled up within her. But she was right, she told herself, and the fact that Spence accepted it only confirmed the truths behind her decision. Whatever else in the world either of them might achieve, they were forbidden each other. Devon blinked back a tear as she faced the brutal reality. But having faced it, her heart cried out at the unfairness that the thing they both loved so deeply, the making of motion pictures, was the sword on which their love should fall.

She stepped out of the bath, wrapping herself in a thick, fluffy towel. Whatever the injustice, she thought, there was nothing she could do about it. And it was rapidly approaching the time when she would have to sit down with Harrison Kahn and lay her cards on the table.

She arrived at Kahn's apartment, in an elegant old building overlooking Central Park, promptly at twelve, and was admitted by a manservant, who ushered her into the study. Harrison was waiting for her; smiling, he squeezed her hand. "Devon," he greeted her, "you look lovely, as usual. Let me give you a sherry."

But his eyes, behind the genial mask, were hard as flint. Devon knew she'd have but one chance and she'd better make it good.

But Kahn seemed in no hurry to get to the problem at hand. Over sherry he questioned her on general studio matters, and soon they adjourned to lunch.

Kahn's manservant had laid a beautiful table and served a succulent sole in clear sauce, then poured a splendid California Riesling. When lunch was done, Kahn lit a cigar, expelling a cloud of blue smoke, and his eyes drilled her. "Now, about *Last Chance*. Have you changed your mind about pulling the plug?"

"I think I can save it," Devon said simply. "And after I explain how, I'm betting you'll agree with me."

Kahn's frown deepened. "You're three million over standing in your shoes right now, Devon. You're telling me you want to chase that with twenty million more." He shook his head. "I'm warning you, it's going to be a tough sell. Particularly with Spence pulling out."

"It will cost six million to shut it down," Devon said quickly. "And we'll have nothing. That's criminal. I could make a good picture for six million."

Kahn eyed her coldly. "Maybe you should have, instead of launching *Last Chance*. As I recall, you're the one who warned me to beware of big-budget fiascos. I must say, this is the last situation I expected to arise when I hired you."

Devon rose to the challenge. "I made a mistake, Harrison. It probably won't be the last one either. But I'm convinced I can bring this picture in for under twenty-three five, and that it's going to recoup enormously at the box office."

Harrison studied her another long moment, his brows furrowed. "All right," he said. "Let's hear it."

Flooded with relief that she would have a chance to make her pitch, Devon quickly ran down the budget figures and then showed Kahn a revised shooting schedule that would lop six days off the distant location. Then she told him about Sean Randall, her choice to replace Kreiss. Kahn was impressed.

"I saw his picture," he said. "Good eye." Then his brow furrowed again. "Still, all of this depends on resuming the shoot on Monday. Four days. You haven't told me about your female lead."

Devon paused. This was the tricky part. Her solution was a daring one; it had come to her in a flash that morning after she'd last spoken with her mother. She wasn't at all sure how Harrison would react.

"I have someone in mind. An actress who's perfect for the part and whose name is very well known. *And* one who will bring a lot of publicity to the picture. I think we can get her for guild minimums and points."

"I think you're living in a fantasy world," Kahn

snapped. "Any actress worth going after will want her money up front!"

Devon smiled. "Oh, I think she'll trust me to see that she's treated fairly."

Kahn's eyes narrowed. "Just who is this paragon of faith in her fellow man?"

"My mother."

Devon had the distinct pleasure of seeing Harrison Kahn thrown for a loop. "What?" he thundered.

Then, even before Devon could elaborate, he frowned, thinking out loud. "There'd be publicity, all right. Sheila O'Neill returns to the screen after twenty years. . . . Plenty of people would come just to see what she looks like now."

"She looks fabulous," Devon said encouragingly.

He nodded. "She'd bring in an older audience, one that's been drifting away from pictures lately. And that youngster Kreiss found will bring in the kids."

"Karl did do one thing right when he cast Jimmy McQuinn," Devon agreed.

Harrison glanced at Devon, and his face broke into a sly smile. "You're Justin O'Neill's daughter, all right. Full of surprises." Then he lapsed back into silence as he mentally weighed his decision. Devon sat nervously on the edge of her chair, her hands clenched tightly in her lap.

Everything depended on the next words Harrison Kahn spoke.

Finally Kahn slapped his thigh and said, "Okay, go ahead. But it'd better not go a nickel over twenty-three five. And I want to see a screen test of your mother before she's cast."

Devon hesitated; her mother hadn't been tested in thirty-five years. Ranking actors and actresses resented screen tests fiercely. But she knew Harrison was right in demanding one.

She sighed. "Okay. We'll test her tomorrow. When do you want to see it?"

Kahn growled, "When you do. I'm flying back out with you tonight."

Devon returned to the Pierre to gather her things for the turnaround flight and to call her mother in Palm Springs. When Sheila answered, Devon took a deep breath. "Mother, how would you like to make a comeback?"

There was stunned silence on the other end of the line, then Sheila asked, "Darling, are you sure you haven't been working too hard?"

Quickly Devon explained her desperate situation, adding with some trepidation, "I have to warn you; Harrison insisted on testing you."

Her mother dismissed the problem breezily. "Oh, that's all right, dear. It won't be the first time." She hesitated, then added, "Well, it's certainly true what they say about connections in the business, isn't it? I only had to wait for you to become president of a studio before my career turned around."

But beneath the teasing banter, Devon sensed excitement.

"Then you'll do it?"

"Of course!"

Devon smiled. "There's one more thing I ought to tell you. By the way Harrison reacted when I mentioned your name, I think he may have a crush on you."

"Devon!" chided her mother. Then she laughed. "Well, that can't hurt when he screens the test, now can it?"

After talking to her mother, Devon phoned the studio and ordered Sheila's test for the next day, a Saturday, which meant a scramble to find a camera crew and technicians to process the film, but finally it was set up.

Two hours later Devon and Harrison Kahn boarded a jet for the flight back out to the coast. Devon knew she ought to feel like she was caught in a revolving door, she'd spent so much time in airplanes recently. But she didn't. She felt like she was on a marvelous merry-go-round, more lighthearted than she'd felt in days.

She'd done it!

Back in Los Angeles, Kahn established himself in his bungalow at the Beverly Hills Hotel while Devon made the final arrangements for her mother's screen test.

The next evening Devon entered the screening room where Harrison Kahn was already waiting. As soon as she sat down she pressed the button on the intercom and told the projectionist to roll the film. In a moment the room was dark, and Sheila O'Neill's still-stunning face filled the screen.

Devon had seen every one of her mother's films many times over and enjoyed them all. But like most people, she had been more aware of her mother's beauty than her acting ability. Now Sheila's mature beauty was matched by acting that had never before been given full reign. In this scene the character she played first teased the hero, then argued angrily with him, then kissed him tenderly.

Watching her mother's performance, Devon felt she was seeing her for the first time. When it was over, her eyes were stinging with tears. To think her mother had always had this ability and had simply never been given a chance. . . .

She glanced at Harrison out of the corner of her eye; he was sitting stock-still. Then he turned to Devon and said in a low voice, "That woman's amazing. It's worth it to me to make this picture just to watch her performance. You can start on Monday."

Devon sighed with relief. Another hurdle was behind her, although she'd never seriously doubted that Harrison would respond. *Last Chance* was alive and well again.

Chapter 21

THE BANFF SHOOT WRAPPED ON TIME AND UNDER BUDGET as the first whiff of spring tinged the air. Devon breathed a huge sigh of relief. The film she was looking at in dailies was marvelous, full of vitality and charged with the epic scope of the sweeping mountain vistas against which it was shot. Her trust in the roaring giant, Sean Randall, had been more than justified. And Sheila was smashing, beyond even Devon's expectations. Accompanied by Harrison Kahn, Devon flew to Banff for the final two days of work on distant location. She was filled with a heady sense of accomplishment; she knew the picture would make a huge impact and rain laurels on all who were responsible. Her emotional state now was a far cry from what it had been on her previous journey to the set of *Last Chance*, when she and Spence were forced to shut down production.

The thought of Spence, as their plane touched down in Calgary, caused her brow to furrow and put a sharp rein on her high spirits. She'd seen almost nothing of him since the picture had resumed shooting. When they met accidentally on the lot, his attitude was stiffly formal, and she adopted the same pose. But beneath her composure her heart pounded mercilessly, and she sensed he was enduring the same ordeal.

Devon had prayed desperately that time would heal the wounds inflicted by their passionate affair. She'd tried to force herself to resume dating, but there was no one in her circle of male acquaintances whom she felt like devoting any time to. Spence, and memories of their time together, burned in her mind. She was only permitted a respite from that torment when she buried herself in her work.

Rebecca warned her that she was gaining a reputation as a celibate and a workaholic. "You've got to play sometime," she chided Devon. "People are beginning to wonder."

Well, let them wonder, Devon thought grimly. But secretly she was beginning to fear that Spence had seared her life with a permanent, indelible brand.

And now he was gone.

He was in London for an indefinite stay as he tried to launch a major new production, a Crimean War epic for which European cofinancing was essential. She felt a stab of pain, remembering that he hadn't bothered to notify her. She'd read about it in the trade papers after he'd already left. Now Devon had no idea which was worse: the emptiness she felt not knowing when she would see him again, or the agony of fearing she would bump into him each time she stepped out of her office.

Harrison Kahn's voice intruded on her thoughts, and she was thankful for the diversion. "I meant to ask, Devon, is your mother still on the schedule, or is she back in LA?" His tone was carefully noncommittal, and Devon suppressed a smile. Kahn could be about as subtle as a pile-driver. He'd spent unprecedented time

on the coast the previous couple of months and had
often shown up at Devon's office about the time rushes
were scheduled. She'd darted glances at him in the
darkened screening room when Sheila's takes were
being shown, and was astonished to realize that she was
watching a helplessly entranced man. It was charming,
she thought, that a mighty entrepreneur like Kahn,
who could make the entertainment world tremble with
a stroke, had fallen prey to her mother's considerable
charms . . . and felt compelled to try to hide his infatu-
ation like a schoolboy.

"She finishes this afternoon," Devon said blandly,
and Kahn's face involuntarily fell. Then she added,
"But she's staying over. I thought the three of us might
all fly back together on Thursday." She arched an
eyebrow. "If that's all right with you?"

"Certainly," he said quickly, and then changed the
subject. But Devon noticed that there was a new spring
in his step when they deplaned, and she smiled with
renewed amazement at love's power to revitalize
human lives.

A company station wagon was waiting for them at
the airport, and by late afternoon they were established
in comfortable suites high in the grand old Banff
Springs Hotel.

That night Devon and Kahn hosted a small supper
party for Sean Randall and the principal cast. Sheila, as
Devon had known she would, made a marvelous
entrance, garbed like a ski bunny in a thick turtleneck
sweater and form-fitting après-ski slacks and looking
nearly as young. For a moment, when she introduced
her mother to Kahn, she feared he wouldn't be able to
utter a word. But Sheila put him instantly at ease,
steering him toward the makeshift bar and mixing him a
drink as if it were *her* party and they'd been old friends
for years.

The supper was an uproarious success. Sean began

by unceremoniously draping his burly arms over Devon's and Harrison Kahn's shoulders and announcing for the benefit of all, "Well, we must be doing something right if these two came all the way up here to feed us and not to lay waste!"

Kahn, flushed by the effects of a couple of drinks and Sheila's attention, laughed, *"So far,* young man. Remember, you haven't wrapped yet."

Devon spotted Sean's young wife, Nora, standing apart from the others, and crossed to her side, smiling. "You should feel very happy. Unless I'm very much mistaken, your husband over there is going to become a major force in the film industry."

"I know," Nora said. Then she turned to Devon with a frown. "I hate to admit it, Devon, but that's what worries me."

So, Devon thought with a sigh, another casualty in the endless struggle of trying to combine love and a career.

"Nora," Devon said carefully, "I want you to know that I was as impressed with your work in the editing room as I was with Sean's. You're not on this picture because you happen to be the director's wife. I mean that, and I want you to remember it."

Nora smiled and squeezed Devon's hand. "Thank you, Devon. I think I needed that tonight."

Later, when Sheila caught her eye, Devon and her mother bade their good nights, Sheila assuring Harrison Kahn that she was indeed looking forward to their flight back to Southern California together.

They adjourned to her mother's rooms, and after ordering hot tea from room service, Devon turned to Sheila. "What is it, Mother? Is there a problem on the picture?"

Sheila laughed. "Certainly not. That Sean Randall is not only a genius but a circus of fun to work with. I've never been on a happier shoot in my life."

"Your own work is nothing short of marvelous." Devon smiled. "You'll get a nomination for sure."

Sheila shook her head, pleased by the compliment. "Darling, you *are* sweet. And prejudiced. Don't get me wrong, I'm not showing false modesty. I think I'm damned good. I can just heart the critics now: 'Miss O'Neill displays a heretofore untapped talent.' But an Oscar . . ."

"And the offers will come pouring in," Devon added. "You're career will be in full swing again."

Sheila nodded, her eyes dancing. "That would be nice. Frankly, although I wouldn't have admitted it for the world, I've had about as much of the pleasures of retirement as I can stand."

She gave Devon a hug. "It *is* fun to think about."

The tea arrived, and after the waiter served them and left, quietly closing the door after himself, Sheila turned to Devon with a concerned frown. "No, Devon, there's no problem on the picture. But I think there may be a problem as far as you're concerned. That's why I wanted to talk."

"Me?"

"Yes. And Spence."

Devon's smile faded. Before she could reply, Sheila continued gently, "I knew something was wrong when I first discovered he was no longer connected with the picture. But you didn't say anything and I didn't want to pry. I was so sure you two would work out whatever was wrong. But it's been over two months, and you haven't mentioned him once. What's happened, Devon?"

Devon's voice went flat. "It's over, Mother. It's that simple."

"It's *not* that simple!" Sheila snapped. "You can't mean that. I saw the way he looked at you at Christmas. The man was in love. And so were you. For the first time in your life."

Remembering that day, Devon had to fight back tears. When she spoke, her voice was infinitely sad. "Love isn't always enough." She shook her head. "But you're right about one thing. It wasn't simple. It was horribly complicated. Being in love and working together just didn't mix."

Sheila sipped her tea thoughtfully. "Believe me, Devon, I do understand. Having it all—a career that demands so much commitment, a marriage, possibly children—isn't easy. Usually something has to give. We all have to make choices. Are you satisfied with yours?"

Devon shook her head sadly. "It wasn't entirely my choice. If it was just a question of my position at the studio, I would have walked away from it, I think, rather than lose Spence. But there was so much more at stake. My own self-esteem. What my success or failure means to other women who are trying to break through the barriers."

Sheila embraced her daughter with affectionate pride, sighing, "My poor baby."

After a moment Devon shook her head firmly. "Enough of this maudlin self-pity. Let's talk about something really interesting." She gave her mother a sly smile. "Remember, I warned you that Harrison might have a crush on you."

Sheila waved her off with a laugh. "Oh, Devon, you don't have any idea what you're talking about."

"Hey, remember who you're working for," she said. "I think a little more respect is in order, even if you did change my diapers." She added, her eyes twinkling, "And I certainly do know what I'm talking about. What's more, I think you're fond of him; I saw the way you took him under your wing."

"I had to . . . he looked so *helpless*," Sheila giggled, then conceded, "He is nice—in a gruff, bulldoggish sort of way."

"Mm, that's what I thought," Devon said. "You know, Mother, I think rejoining the world has done wonders for you, and not just professionally."

Sheila laughed again, showing Devon the door. "What I think is that you'd better keep your busy little nose out of the affairs of your elders."

She gave Devon a peck on the cheek, then said with genuine concern, "I'm sorry I couldn't be of any more help as far as Spence is concerned. I hadn't realized the terrible dilemna you were facing."

"There's nothing anyone can do," Devon said. "I've simply got to put it behind me."

"Sometimes, Devon," her mother cautioned gently, "these things won't stay where you put them."

Later that night Devon turned off the lights in her bedroom and sat at her window, gazing out across the snowfields below, which were almost luminescent in the bright moonlight. She fought the impulse to let her mind dwell on Spence for the million and tenth time, but in his place formed an image that caused her almost as much pain as the memories of her lost love.

Sally.

As she contemplated the snowy landscape she couldn't banish the image of Sally standing in the snow as she and Spence stepped from the four-by, or forget the look of doom in her eyes as she greeted them—the same look that must appear in the eyes of a doe when a hunter's bullet strikes to the heart.

She had no idea where Sally was at that moment. Her friend had left the hospital and vanished without a word or a trace. Devon had no way of knowing even whether she was alive, although she prayed each night that Sally had found some kind of peace.

Devon no longer blamed herself for what had happened to Sally, but she knew in the depths of her heart that her life had touched Sally's and left an imprint.

"No man is an island . . ." said the poet, and it was true. Perhaps if she'd tried harder to reinforce her bridge to Sally's island . . . The thought brought sadness welling up inside of her, and she blinked a tear back from her shining eyes.

Suddenly her longing for Spence became almost unbearable. Oh, yes, Devon thought hopelessly. I do miss you, Spencer Tait. And I'm lonelier tonight than I ever thought it possible to be. There's a continent and an ocean between us, but I feel your presence as though you were in this very room. God, I'd give anything in the world if that were so. . . .

Anything but your ambition, a nagging voice inside her replied.

And she knew it was true.

Chapter 22

WITH COMPLETION OF PRINCIPAL PHOTOGRAPHY, SOME three weeks after the company returned to Los Angeles, *Last Chance* moved into the postproduction phase. It was already late March and—if Devon's goal of a midsummer release was to be realized—the pace of editing, looping and scoring would have to be accelerated incredibly beyond what would normally be the case.

To accommodate Devon's marketing strategy, Sean Randall and his wife moved into a mobile home on the lot, parked adjacent to the row of tiny editing cubicles. Nora supervised three teams of junior editors and assistants under Sean's overall authority, and they worked almost around the clock. During the day Devon ran the studio. But at night she slaved beside Sean and Nora, downing gallons of coffee and staring into the tiny screen of the Moviola, the film editor's basic tool, until her eyes were bleary. She was exhausted from overwork, but it was a labor of love. And besides, exhaustion made it easier to sleep at night. Busy days and nights made it easier to pretend her life was full, even though Spence's love was denied her.

In late May, Devon invited Harrison Kahn to the coast to view a rough cut of *Last Chance*. And on the appointed morning she was only mildly surprised to find Sheila at his side as he strode into her office.

"Surprise, darling!" Sheila laughed, embracing her daughter. "Harrison invited me to the screening, and I was sure you wouldn't mind."

"I'm very pleased, in fact," Devon replied. "I think you'll like what you're going to see." Kahn was standing somewhat self-consciously nearby. Devon linked arms with both of them. "Come on. Sean should be ready for us now." She led them out, secretly thrilled that her mother had finally come out of her self-imposed romantic exile.

When the lights came up in the screening room after the rough cut, Kahn turned to Devon. "I don't pretend to have my finger on the public pulse, Devon—that's what I pay you for—but as far as I'm concerned, that's one hell of a movie."

"It's going to be marvelous, darling," Sheila said, squeezing Devon's hand, and she could see tears glistening in her mother's eyes.

"*You* were marvelous," Harrison Kahn said warmly to Sheila, and once again Devon was touched at the guileless devotion he displayed for her. And the intimate warmth in the smile her mother offered in return left little doubt that their relationship had progressed considerably beyond where it had left off at Banff.

"I'm glad you both feel that way," Devon said, getting down to business. "I'm very pleased with it myself, so much so that I'd like to premier it at Radio City Music Hall on July first."

Harrison hesitated, then grinned broadly. "Why not? Might as well shoot for the moon. Let's face those New

York critics and get it over with. Can the ad campaign and marketing strategy be ready by then?"

"They'll be ready," Devon said confidently.

Later, when her mother had stepped into the powder room in Devon's spacious office, Kahn turned to Devon with a serious expression.

"Devon, I don't suppose I have to tell you that your job is riding on this picture."

"You don't have to tell me."

He fidgeted awkwardly a moment. "I suppose it's no secret that I . . . ah, enjoy your mother's company?"

"No," she agreed, "it's no secret."

"What I'm trying to say, damn it," he erupted in frustration, "is that that won't have any bearing on my decision about your future with UFS if *Last Chance* goes down the drain. It can't! I have a responsibility to the board of directors and the shareholders of the company." He swallowed. "Even if firing you costs me your mother's affection."

"Just so that you understand my position, Harrison," Devon said frowning, "let me make it clear that if the picture fails, I won't wait around to be fired. You have nothing to worry about on that score."

He eyed her critically for a moment. "You know, when I hired you, Devon, I never had any doubt that you were smart and a straight shooter. But I wondered if you were tough enough. And frankly at the time I doubted if you were. But we were in a bind at the time, with the embezzlement and all, and I had to have somebody in a hurry, so I gambled."

"And now you regret it?" Devon asked. "Is that what you're trying to tell me?"

"Not at all," Kahn said gently. "What I'm trying to tell you is that I've noticed a change in you these last few months. The job's toughened you in a way I was hoping it would. Whichever way *Last Chance* falls, you took charge and followed your star. I admire that."

So she was tough now, Devon thought to herself with mixed emotions. Well, losing the love of her life and watching a close friend flirt perilously with death would probably toughen most people, if they survived. The question, of course, remained: Was it worth it? And Devon had profound doubts.

But for Kahn's benefit she smiled. "Thank you. That means a lot to me."

Later, as she was seeing Kahn and Sheila off, her mother took her aside. "Darling," she said with concern, "I couldn't say anything earlier, but you must ease up. You look utterly exhausted. I know you have terrible responsibilities just now, but nothing is *that* important. You can't let these things destroy you."

Devon smiled wryly. "Harrison says I'm tough."

"Oh, he's a moron!" Sheila exclaimed. "Sweet, but still a man. Ladies are not tough; competent and organized, yes, but never tough."

Devon laughed. "I'll try to remember that."

Her mother gave her an inquiring look. "And Spence?"

Devon merely shook her head.

Her mother sighed. "I'm sorry. But I still believe that's going to work out. Somehow."

"And you?"

Her mother gave a girlish laugh. "We're going on to Maui for a few days. Harrison has a house there." She winked mischievously. "Very 'today' of me, don't you think?"

Devon hugged Sheila. "I think it's marvelous. And you look so happy."

Devon watched the limousine wheel away through the front gates of the studio, past the guardhouse, and onto Hollywood Boulevard. She was happy for her mother, but she was afraid Sheila was wrong on two counts. Ladies might be all that she described, but if one of them wanted to be head of a studio, that lady had better be tough as hell. And as far as Spence was concerned, all her mother's optimism could never breathe life back into their love.

A week or so later Devon was sitting on a dubbing stage with Sean and their composer, scoring the picture, once again totally immersed in her work. A beautiful score had been written, warm and moving for the heroine's theme and broadly powerful with tragic *Twilight of the Gods* undertones for the action sequences, which had been shot against the epic backdrop of the Canadian Rockies. Devon couldn't have been more pleased, and Sean was ecstatic.

"Wagnerian, by God!" he boomed. "That's what it is! Give me a maniac every time!"

It was then Devon glanced up from her production notes . . . and froze.

Sally was standing in the doorway.

Quickly Devon excused herself and rushed to her friend's side.

"Sally—!"

"Hi," she said, smiling tentatively.

Suddenly Devon couldn't hold back her emotion; she embraced Sally fiercely, flooded with relief that she was alive and well. "Why on earth didn't you telephone . . . or write . . . or *something?*"

"I couldn't," Sally said, her eyes glistening with tears. "Dev, I just couldn't. Not after what I'd done to you."

Devon managed a smile. "Come on, let's get out of here for a while."

They adjourned to a coffee shop opposite the studio, and once they'd settled into a secluded rear booth, Devon demanded, "What happened to you?"

Sally shook her head. "I had to get away. I knew I couldn't face anyone, particularly after you were so wonderful about offering to take me back to the studio."

"Oh, Sally, I was so afraid I'd driven you away."

"Uh-uh. In fact, your support was the only thing that kept me on my feet." She smiled.

"Where did you go?"

"Everywhere. Nowhere. I just started driving. I decided to keep going until I found a place that felt right and then stop for a while." She smiled. "It turned out to be Santa Fe."

"Santa Fe!"

"I know, it seems so remote from here. But it was beautiful . . . the mountains and high desert. Well, to shorten the story, I rented a little house in the country and began to see a psychologist."

"About Karl? And what happened?"

Sally nodded. "You were right. After a while things didn't seem so black anymore. And I learned so much about myself." She shook her head. "The truth is, I'm not as strong as you are, Devon. This business, making pictures, can be incredibly destructive. You seem to be able to hold yourself apart from the destructive elements of it. I can't . . . it swallows me up."

"Sally, you're back. That's the important thing. And your job is still there. As far as being swallowed up, well, we just won't let that happen again."

"No"—Sally smiled gently—"it won't happen again. Because I'm not staying, Devon." She met Devon's eyes almost apologetically. "You see, I met a man. A rancher. Not exactly the Ma Maison type, but what I'm looking for, what I need. He's a widower with two small children. Devon, I'm incredibly in love."

I should have known, Devon thought. The radiant excitement in Sally's eyes was self-explanatory. She squeezed Sally's hand with genuine happiness for her friend. "I think that's wonderful, Sally."

"Then you're not disappointed in me?"

"Disappointed?" Devon said with dismay. "Sally, I envy you!"

A puzzled frown crossed Sally's face. "You envy *me?* I was afraid you'd think I was silly, throwing away a career."

Devon smiled gently. "If he's got two small children, I suspect you're just beginning a career. I understand the role of stepmother is as tough as line-producing."

They chatted for more than an hour. Sally was bubbling over with excitement about her new life in Santa Fe, the magnificent landscapes, the theatre and concert opportunities and her love for the strong, quiet cattleman who was taking her away from the racking business of picture-making.

And Sally was right to put it behind her, Devon thought. The film industry, with all the pressure, heartache, fast people and fast money would eventually have destroyed her. That or made her life a lingering misery. Hollywood wasn't for everyone. Talent wasn't enough. You had to be strong.

And tough, she added as an afterthought.

Later, she bade Sally good-bye, promising that she and Rebecca both would make the trip to Santa Fe for the wedding. And as she walked back to the dubbing stage to continue work on *Last Chance,* passing Spence's empty parking space behind the executive offices, she realized that she hadn't merely been trying to bolster Sally's commitment to her new life and love.

Devon did envy her. She envied her desperately.

Chapter 23

SPENCE STOOD AT THE SMALL, WELL-STOCKED BAR IN HIS suite at Blakes Hotel and poured himself a stiff brandy. He had wanted to avoid this hotel. But it was the height of the London tourist season and there was nothing else available that was decent.

"I'll have Scotch if you've got it, love. A little soda, no ice."

The voice was aristocratic, low-key, entirely feminine.

Spence mixed the drink, then carried it over to the rumpled bed, where a young woman lay only partially covered by a sheet.

She *is* gorgeous, Spence thought objectively. A lush body that might have come straight out of a Botticelli painting. Perfect features and classic bone structure. Mahogany hair and clear blue eyes. . . .

Just like Devon.

Spence swallowed the brandy in a single gulp. But she wasn't Devon. For the first time all evening he squarely faced the fact that he'd taken this girl to bed because she reminded him of Devon.

It was a mistake he regretted bitterly now. It was stupid to have even hoped that he could exorcise Devon's ghost by trying to find a look-alike replacement.

Her name was Holly Gregson and she was an English actress who hoped for a role in Spence's Crimean epic.

We've used each other tonight, Spence thought without any feelings of bitterness toward Holly. She was merely being practical. And who knows, maybe she even found me attractive. My motivation is a hell of a lot worse than hers.

Pulling the belt on his robe a bit tighter, Spence looked her straight in the eye. "You've got the part. Tell your agent to call me." She looked momentarily startled, then pleased. "I'd rather you left now," he finished quietly.

A few minutes later she was dressed and gone.

Spence sat in a chair, sipping his third brandy. Holly was a lousy actress, but he felt he owed her the part. He would tell the writer to cut her lines to the minimum; she would get by on her magnificent looks.

The question was, how would he get by? He wondered.

As he'd driven into London from Heathrow Airport he had told himself the city would have no effect on him. He and Devon hadn't left an indelible imprint on it. But he was wrong. Everything he saw reminded him of her and of the night they had spent there that changed his life forever.

He sighed heavily and leaned his blond head against the tall back of the chair. He was unutterably weary of episodes like that night's. At first he had actively sought out brief liaisons in the desperate hope that they would dull his memories of making love to Devon. It hadn't worked, of course. Nothing did.

It was amusing in a way, he thought. At least the women he had known would find it so. Spencer Tait, who had gone through affairs, not so much with conscious cruelty but a decided lack of concern, was hooked. Irrevocably. Hopelessly.

He finished the last drop of brandy in the glass. And gazed into a future that was bleak indeed, because Devon wasn't in it. . . .

Chapter 24

A WEEK BEFORE IT WAS DUE TO PREMIERE, A FULL-PAGE ad for *Last Chance* ran in the New York *Times* at a cost of $27,000. Another $24,000 was spent to book Radio City Music Hall, and another $50,000 for a blitz of radio and television spots in the New York metropolitan market. But, Devon thought with satisfaction, the cost of framing the premiere properly, considering its importance to the ultimate success of the picture, was insignificant. The two performances were sold out, with eleven thousand paid tickets for each of the two performances. In addition the studio was flying in critics from key outlying areas, lodging them in the best hotels and staging a postscreening gala at the Waldorf for all concerned. The gala was replete with major entertainment, stars, and a gourmet buffet. All the hoopla that Hollywood press agentry could muster was brought to bear on the launching of *Last Chance*. Devon was satisfied that she'd done everything humanly possible for her picture.

Backstage at seven, Devon waited with Harrison and Sheila, making nervous small talk. Both women had dressed to the hilt on this crucial night. Devon was stunning in a flowing lavender gown in the sheerest chiffon over silk. But Sheila was even more glamorous, every inch the movie star, in a narrow, ankle-length skirt and matching dolman-sleeved pullover in metallic black velour chiffon.

It had been an extremely hectic week. They hadn't finished mixing the sound for the movie until the previous day. Final negative changes were completed the previous night, and Devon had brought the master print with her from the coast when she flew in that morning.

Sean Randall joined them, looking a bit incongruous in a tuxedo, his massive shoulders straining the seams of his jacket. He was delighted. "I love this place! Look at that screen. You could cover the Astrodome with it!"

Devon smiled. "The ratio is one-point-three-to-one. One and a third times as wide as it is high. That was the original ratio for motion pictures back in Griffith's day."

Sean snorted good-naturedly. "You would know something like that. That's why you're the boss and I'm the flunky."

"Some flunky," Devon laughed.

"Anyway, it's big. It will do the picture justice." He nodded with satisfaction.

Devon fidgeted nervously. She wished they would get on with the screening. The audience, those final arbiters of all the blood, sweat and tears that had gone into the making of *Last Chance,* was in place, and now she was desperate to hear the verdict, good or bad.

As the lights began to dim, they slipped into the theatre and were shown to their seats near the rear of the auditorium. The picture began, and suddenly Devon realized she wouldn't be able to endure sitting there. Excusing herself in a whisper, she got up and returned to the lobby. She waited there, occasionally opening the aisle door to listen for audience reaction and drawing stern frowns from the ushers. But she could make no judgment about how the film was being received.

Then it was over. There was a moment of silence . . . and then, as one, the audience exploded into applause and cheers, and Devon's heart soared!

Feeling as light as a feather, Devon hastened from the lobby as the excited audience began spilling out of the auditorium.

She was joined in a large rehearsal studio backstage by Sean, Sheila and the other principal cast members. A press conference had been set up, and the triumphant picture-makers were arrayed along a table covered with microphones as newsmen and critics fired questions. Devon's long-held phobia concerning publicity evaporated; this wasn't an ordeal, it was a love feast. Most of the questions were directed at Sheila, the clear hit of the evening. Devon was vaguely aware of Harrison standing unobtrusively in the back of the hall, watching proudly as her mother parried and bantered enchantingly with the media.

With the press conference over, all adjourned for the Waldorf and the celebration. But Harrison Kahn managed to pull Devon aside for a moment.

"You did it," he congratulated.

"Does that mean I still have my job?" she countered with a laugh.

"I might even be willing to renegotiate your contract upward," Kahn said, his eyes twinkling, "if someone were to ask me."

"Is that my cue?" Rebecca laughed, joining them. She embraced Devon happily. "I'll be glad to go to bat for Devon."

"Listen, both of you," Devon said firmly. "If we've got a hit on our hands, it was because a lot of different people worked their hearts out—"

But Kahn dismissed that with a wave of his hand. "I warned you about false modesty. Devon, *you* kept this picture going when everyone else, myself included, thought it ought to be rolled up. By God, you showed better instincts than Spencer Tait, and that's saying something." He gave her a fatherly kiss on the cheek. "You're the belle of this ball, my dear, and don't you forget it. Now, I'll see you at the party. I believe your mother is waiting for me."

Devon wandered into the empty lobby. Suddenly she didn't feel like going to the party just yet. Instead she went back into the theatre.

It was empty by then. Without an audience and a film, it was only another huge, empty room. It only came alive when fantasy was in the air.

She sat down for a quiet moment. She felt immensely relieved. As Harrison said, she had believed in the picture all along. Through thick and thin she'd clung to her convictions. And she was proud of her triumphant vindication.

But she wasn't happy. And she knew perfectly well why. Without Spence it was a hollow victory.

"Is this seat taken?"

Startled, Devon looked up into the greenest eyes in the world. Spence stood there, one hand thrust casually into the pocket of his black tuxedo while an ironic smile played at the corners of his mouth.

"You were here tonight?" she managed to whisper.

"Of course. I wouldn't have missed the biggest night of your life. I flew over from London this morning."

He sat down beside her. As he looked earnestly into her eyes Devon felt her heart melt. "It was fantastic, Devon. I don't know how you did it, but you turned it around completely. You took a disaster and made it a stunning success. I was wrong."

"No, you weren't. It might just as well have turned out the other way. Then you'd have lost everything you've worked so hard for."

"If it had happened that way, I couldn't have felt any worse than I've felt without you these past few months."

Those were the sweetest words she'd ever heard. Sweeter than all the applause, than the critics' compliments. Sweeter by far than Harrison's offer of a new contract.

She didn't have to say she felt the same. It was achingly obvious in the way her love for him shone in her azure eyes.

"Are you coming to the party?" she asked.

His expression clouded. "No. I'm flying back to London on the red-eye. I thought it best . . ."

His voice trailed off and he looked away.

He was right, she knew. It was madness for them to be together, even for a few brief moments. But despite the awful, wrenching pain she knew she'd feel when he left, she was glad he'd come. Just to see him again, to hear that he missed her as terribly as she missed him, made it all worthwhile.

"Well . . ." The word hung in the air.

Devon rose and Spence followed.

"I'd better go now," she said. "They'll be waiting."

"I'll walk you outside to a taxi."

She nodded.

Outside, the hot summer night was in stark contrast to the coolness of the air-conditioned theatre.

As Spence handed Devon into the back of a cab, he said, "Good-bye, Devon."

A world of unexpressed feelings were in the brief words.

"Good-bye, Spence."

As the taxi drove off, Devon leaned back against the seat.

"Hot night, ain't it?" the driver said conversationally.

But it wasn't the stifling heat that caused the terrible lump in Devon's throat.

Chapter 25

DEVON STARED OUT OVER THE GREEN GROVES OF ORANGE trees at the dusty summer-brown fields beyond. It was evening, and a magnificent sunset of burnt orange, gold and crimson filled the sky.

She'd come back to her grandparents' ranch because she needed desperately to get away from Hollywood for a while. Now, as she sat cross-legged on the low brow of a hill, she knew the retreat hadn't worked. Being there only reminded her of Spence and a time when they were as close as two people can ever dream of being.

Tears stung her eyes, but she was determined not to give in to them. She couldn't spend the rest of her life crying, she told herself.

Suddenly the silence of her lonely hilltop was broken by a sound. Turning, she saw someone walking toward her. The sun was in her eyes, though, and she couldn't quite make out the male figure. Shading her eyes with one hand, she looked again. What she saw now made her heart stop and her tears disappear.

It was Spence.

She stood there, waiting for him, as he walked purposefully toward her. She had no idea what he was doing there, how he had known where to find her. It didn't matter. All that mattered was that he was here, now.

When he reached her, he stopped and stared at her for a long moment. The love in his eyes was so naked, so vulnerable, that she wanted to turn away in embarrassment. But she didn't. She looked back at him, glorying in his presence, in the love he felt for her.

Ignoring explanations, he began, "I couldn't stay away any longer. I have something for you. I picked it up in London, but it came from South Africa."

From his pocket he took a tiny black velvet box. Devon didn't have to open it to know what it contained. It was large enough for only one thing. A ring.

But, opening the box, she found it to be a ring like no other she'd ever seen. A huge diamond solitaire, at least five carats, set in platinum. It wasn't the size that was so stunning. It was the color. It was pink—a flawless natural pink diamond, brilliantly cut.

As Devon raised her eyes to look at Spence, too stunned to speak, he said softly, "I told you once, pink is for girls."

Her heart was in her throat. She was so filled with love, she thought she would burst.

"Marry me, Devon. Please."

I want to, she thought. Oh, God, I want to so much I can hardly bear it.

Her life was meaningless without him, empty and devoid of joy.

Still holding the tiny box, she placed her hands on his broad chest and looked into his green, green eyes. The love she saw there was so naked, so vulnerable, that everything else paled in comparison. She felt her heart quiver, then melt with tenderness. Love ravished her heart and mind together and she knew the chasm between them was breached once and for all.

"I don't know what will happen to us when we leave this hilltop," she whispered. "I only know that none of the problems facing us matter compared to what I feel for you. Spence, I've been torn for so long, but now I know my mind and my heart. The success of *Last Chance*, my job, *nothing* matters if I'm so desperately unhappy without you."

With a newfound serenity in her voice, she finished, "I love you more than anything in life."

Fiercely he gathered her into his arms and pulled her against him. "Darling, darling Devon." His lips brushed her forehead and she could feel his heart pounding in his chest.

After a moment, he released her, then smiled into her eyes. "Maybe you don't have to give up everything. I have an idea—one I've been thinking about for some time. It's obvious you and I work well together. There's a special kind of synergism with us. Together we're better than we are apart. And we're certainly happier.

"So . . ." He took a deep breath, then forged ahead. "I want us to form an independent production company together. Eventually it would be a studio, if all goes well. Our *own* studio. You'd be my partner. And my wife. Between us, we can make the kind of marvelous pictures we both dream of, with complete control from development to distribution."

Devon hesitated. It was a bold idea, something she'd never even considered before. She and Spence would both be giving up something. He would give up the security of working through UFS. She would give up her status as head of the studio. But, on the other hand, she would have a great deal more freedom. . . .

"I discussed the idea with a banker at Chase Manhattan. Strictly in private, of course. He said we could probably have an immediate line of credit of about forty million. That's not much compared to UFS standards, I know, but . . ."

His voice trailed off as he watched her face. Then he finished, "There will still be problems. But we'll work them out."

Suddenly Devon remembered his own words about making dreams come true: "I have to try. Even if I run the risk of losing everything. Because if I don't try for it, I've lost anyway."

And, besides, I've always enjoyed a challenge, she thought, as a slow smile lit her face. And there would be very special rewards.

Spence's piercing green eyes looked into her blue ones.

"Well?" he breathed huskily. The barely checked passion in his look sent a thrill up her spine.

"Yes. You know as well as I do that only happy endings are allowed in Hollywood," she whispered.

Then she slipped her arms around his neck as his lips met hers.

Silhouette Intimate Moments

Available Now

Raven's Prey by Stephanie James

Honor Knight had to convince Judd Raven the two men who
had hired him to find her weren't her father and brother.
Only Honor hadn't realized Judd was holding her prisoner
for his own reason: he was in love.

Against The Rules by Linda Howard

At seventeen Cathryn Ashe had fought Rule Jackson and lost.
Now, more sure of herself and her new-found independence,
she was ready to challenge him again—only this time,
her heart was at stake.

The Fires Of Winter by Beverly Bird

As editor of a small paper, Heather Cavelle tried to write only
of the good in the world. Then David Sullivan took over and
plunged the paper into a search for crime and hidden truths,
and what they discovered was their love for each other.

Fantasies by Pamela Wallace

When Spencer Tait met the new studio president
Devon O'Neill they clashed immediately. Tensions were high
and the future at stake as the cameras rolled—because this
time, the real story was taking place behind the scenes.

Genuine Silhouette
sterling silver bookmark
for only $15.95!

What a beautiful way to hold your place in your current romance! This genuine sterling silver bookmark, with the distinctive Silhouette symbol in elegant black, measures 1½″ long and 1″ wide. It makes a beautiful gift for yourself, and for every romantic you know! And, at only $15.95 each, including all postage and handling charges, you'll want to order several now, while supplies last.

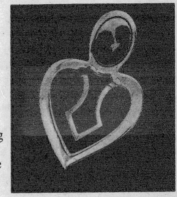

Send your name and address with check or money order for $15.95 per bookmark ordered to

Simon & Schuster Enterprises
120 Brighton Rd., P.O. Box 5020
Clifton, N.J. 07012
Attn: Bookmark

Bookmarks can be ordered pre-paid only. No charges will be accepted. Please allow 4-6 weeks for delivery.

N.Y. State Residents
Please Add Sales Tax

Silhouette Intimate Moments

Coming Next Month

This Magic Moment by Nora Roberts

Pierce Atkins was a magician skilled at escaping the canniest traps and evading the dangerously seductive net of emotion. But Ryan Swan was determined to prove to him that her love was no illusion.

Old Love, New Love by Jane Clare

Three years had gone by since Kee had loved Tobin— and left him. Now she knew that a man like Tobin Furnival came along only once in a woman's life, but was it a lesson learned too late?

Diana's Folly by Jillian Blake

Covering the Kentucky Derby was especially exciting for Diana Jennings because she had the inside track on an exclusive story. But then fellow reporter Beau Gatling arrived on the scene and Diana risked her story for an exclusive on love.

Waltz In Scarlet by Muriel Bradley

From the moment Christina Chandler began to inventory the Fabrian estate she fell under the spell of one of its heirs, Matthew Warden—and into his arms for stolen nights of passion.